'You're here on a working holiday, looking for work in the vineyard?'

Nick was offering Sarah an escape route. But suppose she was to be found out? What if he was to discover that she was a liar and a cheat?

It would only be for the summer, whispered the tiny voice of temptation. Then I'll go back to England and no one here will ever know.

Dear Reader

For many of us, this is the best period of the year—the season of goodwill and celebration—though it can make big demands on your time and pocket, too! Or maybe you prefer to spend these mid-winter months more quietly? Whatever you've got planned, Mills & Boon's romances are always there for you as special friends at the turn of the year: easy, entertaining and comforting reads that are great value for money. Stay warm, won't you!

The Editor

Gloria Bevan was born in Kalgoorlie Australia but went to New Zealand at an early age. As she lived in small towns she wrote for local farming magazines. Mystery novels followed. Author Essie Summers introduced her to Mills & Boon and the magical world of romance writing. She now lives in Auckland with its glorious harbour, bush-covered hills and sandy beaches. She has three daughters, two cats and is fond of reading, travelling—and friends!

SUMMER'S VINTAGE

BY

GLORIA BEVAN

MILLS & BOON LIMITED
ETON HOUSE 18-24 PARADISE ROAD
RICHMOND SURREY TW9 1SR

First published in Great Britain in 1992
by Mills & Boon Limited

This edition 1993

ISBN 0 263 77860 6

Set in Times Roman 10 on 11½ pt
01-9301-52457 C

Made and printed in Great Britain

CHAPTER ONE

'I GOT your letter asking me to call in and see you.' Sarah's eyes were dark with puzzlement as she glanced across the width of the office desk at the plump, balding man facing her.

'Glad you came.' The solicitor's shrewd gaze appraised her. A slim girl of medium height, creamy skin with a dusting of freckles across her nose, thick dark brown hair cut straight across her forehead. Not strictly beautiful by today's standards, and yet—— There was something about her that held him, an air of freshness and vitality. The absurd thought crossed his mind that her smile, wide and warm and friendly, flashed like a ray of summer sunshine in the dingy office surroundings.

'Honestly,' she was saying, 'I can't imagine why you would want to see *me*. There must be some mistake.'

An appealing voice too, he told himself, soft yet clear, and wondered how she would react to the information he was about to impart to her. Aloud he murmured enquiringly, 'You are Miss Smith? Sarah Smith?'

'Oh, yes, that's me. Look.' Reaching into her shoulder-bag, she drew out a folded paper. 'I've brought my birth certificate as you asked me to. Although of course——' once again the captivating smile broke across her face '—no one ever calls me by that name nowadays.'

'Indeed?' His tone had sharpened. 'And why is that?'

'Why?' A trill of laughter bubbled from her lips. 'How would you like to be lumbered with a name like Smith?

I mean, they're two a penny. So,' she confided, 'when I moved away from London and went to live with my aunt in Devon I decided to do something about it. Ever since then I've used my mother's name of Sinclair. A big improvement on plain old Smith, wouldn't you say?'

'Quite, quite.' Sarah realised he wasn't listening, his attention centred on the papers lying on the desk in front of him. He cleared his throat. 'According to information I've received from a law firm out in New Zealand, they've been trying to locate your whereabouts for a considerable length of time—over a year, actually. It seems they've only just been able to trace you at your aunt's address in Devon. Your change of name——'

'My name?' Sarah's green eyes glimmered with amusement. 'Why? Does it make any difference?'

He said drily, 'Quite a lot, actually, seeing there's a matter of a legacy. I have to inform you,' the impressive legal tones went on, 'that under the will of the late Steven Juravich——'

'Steven?' Sarah's eyes widened in shock and dismay. She said on a quick indrawn breath, 'You're not telling me that he—— He's not——?'

As he took in the sudden pallor of her face, the solicitor's tone softened. 'His death was sudden.'

'Not Steven,' she whispered dazedly, for the staggering news seemed to her to be beyond credence. 'He was so big and strong. He couldn't have died.'

He said gently, 'He suffered a massive heart attack. Believe me, it happens more often than you'd imagine, even to men who are only in their late thirties, as he was.'

Still she seemed unable to take in what he was telling her.

He prompted quietly, 'You knew Steven Juravich well?'

'Yes—no—that is——' Sarah moistened dry lips. 'It was only for a few weeks here in London.' She seemed to have difficulty in concentrating. 'It was—oh, ages ago. I was only a child of eleven. Steven and Kathy, my sister, were engaged to be married, only——' Her voice thickened and died into silence.

Tilting back his swivel-chair, the solicitor crossed his legs and eyed her attentively. 'Tell me about it, about them.'

'There's not much to tell.' She made an effort to collect her whirling thoughts. 'It was one of those chance meetings, you know? Steven came from New Zealand. He'd been touring around Europe and on his way home he broke his journey for a few weeks' stopover in London. One day he happened to walk into the souvenir store where Kathy was working. They got talking and he asked her if she'd be his guide and show him around the city.' Her expressionless tones were those of a girl speaking in a dream.

'In Europe he'd only been interested in vineyards. You see, he owned a vineyard back home in New Zealand, and climatic conditions were almost the same as on the Mediterranean. He'd inherited the vineyard from his grandfather who'd brought the original vines from the Dalmatian coast when he settled in New Zealand. Steve said he wanted to plant new varieties of grapes, specialise in a few top varieties, and the places he had visited in Europe had been ever so helpful to him, showed him how to bring his methods up to date in his own vineyard.

'It sounds silly,' the deadpan voice ran on, 'but he and Kathy fell in love almost at first sight, they really did. He had only three weeks to stay in London before he was due to return home in time to get his vines planted at the right season of the year. He'd be back in London in three months' time, he promised Kathy. It would take him that length of time to have a new home built on the property in place of the old cottage he lived in. He wanted everything at Sunvalley to be perfect for her when he brought her there as his bride. But...' Her voice faltered and the solicitor had to strain to catch the low tones. 'It didn't happen that way.' A tape rolled back and across the screen of memory flickered a scene at Heathrow Airport. Kathy and Steven, their last goodbye. Her practical, no-nonsense sister in an abandonment of weeping, clinging compulsively to the big, tanned man who held her close...

'I can't let you go.'

'It won't be for long, my love. A few short months,' he had murmured brokenly, 'then we'll be together again, have the rest of our lives to make up for this. A whole new life together.'

It wasn't *fair*, the child Sarah had been had told herself rebelliously over and over again in the dark days that followed, for Kathy to have been killed before she had had her marriage to Steven—or anything.

The solicitor's voice broke the silence. 'What happened?'

'Kathy was killed in a road accident on the way to the airport. She was leaving London that day for New Zealand.' Sarah swallowed. 'A drunken driver, a car out of control hit them head-on. They were both killed outright—Kathy and our mother.'

'Your mother too?' He was shocked from his complacency. For once in his professional life he could find no words of comfort to offer. After a moment his quiet tones broke across her agonised rememberings. 'You haven't forgotten him, then, this Steven?'

'Forget Steven?' All at once her toneless accents were fraught with emotion. 'You don't forget a man like him! You just couldn't. Steven was special. His face and arms and neck were so deeply tanned, you wouldn't believe. It came from working outside in the open, tending the vines all year round, he told us. He had a trimmed black beard and a deep, gravelly voice, and he was so—sort of caring. I used to hope that some day when I was grown up I'd find someone to love me—a man like him.' A fugitive smile touched her lips. 'I guess he was my ideal.'

The solicitor cleared his throat. 'Tell me, did you correspond with Steven?'

'Only for a while. I guess you couldn't call it corresponding. I used to write him letters telling him about school grades, my sports team—all that stuff. He wouldn't really have been interested in a kid like me. For the last few years I've sent him a card at Christmas time, but he never sent one back to me. I expect he'd forgotten all about me.'

'I see.' The lawyer regarded his pen thoughtfully. 'You haven't a father living, I take it?'

Sarah shook her head. 'He left the family when I was so young, I don't even remember him.'

'So,' he pursued, 'your only relative is your aunt?'

'Oh, yes!' All at once her soft tones were animated. 'She's a pet. I think the world of her.'

'So after the accident,' he probed gently, 'you went to live with your aunt?'

'That's right.' Pushing aside the dark memories that still had power to haunt her, Sarah lifted her chin and said with spirit, 'I owe her a lot!'

'No doubt.' Clearly he had lost interest in her family history, such as it was. And really you couldn't blame him, she thought ruefully. Twenty years of age and a virgin, she didn't even have a torrid love-affair to lend colour to the narrative. For you couldn't count the young men who had asked her out and later proved to be of no interest to her—lukewarm affairs of brief duration and as swiftly forgotten.

She wrinkled her nose at him. 'Not a very exciting life story, is it?'

'It will be.' She caught an enigmatic note in his voice. 'Believe me, Miss Smith, it will be.'

'Sarah——' she corrected.

'I don't think, Sarah, you've quite taken in what I've been trying to tell you. Under the terms of the will you stand to inherit a considerable sum of money, mainly invested in New Zealand banks and the stock-market. In all...' He named a figure that made her gasp. 'In addition——' she brought her mind back to his clipped legal tones '—there's a property of considerable value, a vineyard situated in New Zealand in a district named... named——' He broke off, peering through his bifocals at the unfamiliar word in the document before him.

'Waimarie,' she put in promptly. 'It's a Maori name and it means "a good omen". Steven told me all about it and he showed me pictures of the vineyard. It's in a valley, and the hills all around are so densely covered with native bush that light planes that have gone down there have never been found. It——'

'Yes, yes,' the solicitor cut in impatiently. 'Evidently a remotely situated property even in New Zealand, where I understand there are vast tracts of bush and farmlands between settlements.'

'You said Steven had left his beloved vineyard to me?' Sarah was staring at him in disbelief. 'I don't understand.'

'Let me explain. It seems that Steven Juravich's will was drawn up in London many years ago in favour of your sister, whom he regarded as his future wife. Under the terms of the will, in the event of her death the estate passed to her nearest relative—you, her sister.'

Sarah's eyes were thoughtful as she pursued the matter to its logical conclusion. 'Steven hadn't ever married, then? Or had any children or relatives?'

He didn't answer the question directly. Past experience of similar bequests had led him to take a somewhat pessimistic view in these matters, but maybe this girl would be lucky. Aloud he murmured, 'Apparently not. There are certain bequests to residents in New Zealand but, according to the information I've been given, Steven was an only child and a bachelor.'

To change the subject he said smoothly, 'The capital left to you in the will will not be available for some time, but meantime I can let you have an advance drawn on Sunvalley estate.'

'Could you really do that?' Her face was alive with wonder. 'That would be great!'

The solicitor discussed further details of the inheritance and produced papers for her to sign, while in her dazed state of mind Sarah tried to make herself believe that all this was really happening. 'Tell me,' the dry masculine tones broke across her confused thoughts, 'how much would you like to go on with? Say a few thousand?'

Had he actually mentioned 'thousands'? She said quickly, 'Oh, I just need enough money to cover my return fare out to New Zealand. I'd better have a bit extra for living expenses when I get there.'

He sent her a sharp, enquiring glance. 'You're not thinking of taking a trip out to the vineyard?'

'But of course I am!' She stared at him incredulously. 'I can't *wait* to see the property for myself! I want to stay there a while—say for three months—get to know the workings of the vineyard, find out all I can about it.'

He returned his swivel-chair to an upright position with an exasperated jerk. 'If I could make a suggestion...' He couldn't quite conceal the annoyance in his tone. 'In situations like this it's better not to rush things. If you insist on going to see this property——'

'Oh, I do! I do! I can't *wait*——' Sarah's eyes were shining with enthusiasm.

The lawyer's lips tightened disapprovingly, but he knew when he was beaten. 'I could see to your travel arrangements, arrange for someone to be at the airport in Auckland to meet you on arrival in New Zealand. The vineyard is evidently in a remote area. It might be difficult for you to get there without making prior arrangements.'

She was undeterred. 'But I know just where it is on the map.'

'All the same,' he demurred, 'there could be nowhere for you to stay when you reach the place.'

'But of course there will be.' Her voice rang with confidence. 'Steven has been living there for years. He must have a housekeeper—or someone. And there's bound to be a manager taking care of the vineyard meanwhile. Anyway——' the dancing look was back in her eyes '—I'll take a chance on it!'

'At least,' he persisted, 'you'll let me inform the vineyard people of your expected arrival date, flight number and so on?'

'Why should I?' He realised she had the bit between her teeth and there was no holding her back. 'That's half the fun. It's going to be a surprise!'

I'll bet it will! He said the words silently.

Suddenly her laughing face sobered and the excitement died out of her eyes. 'You won't tell them I'm coming out to New Zealand?' He caught the note of urgency in her tones. 'You won't, will you? *Please*,' she begged.

He hesitated, and she seized the advantage. 'Couldn't you let things go along as they are just for a little while longer? I mean, there must be someone at the vineyard keeping things going at the moment.'

'There is, actually,' he told her. 'A manager who's been there for some time.'

'Do me a favour, then. Let him get on with his job.' Sensing his disapproval, she urged persuasively, 'Couldn't you tell the lawyers in New Zealand that you've contacted me and you'll get in touch with them later? Just don't let them know I'm coming.'

'If that's what you want,' he murmured reluctantly.

'Oh, it is! It is! Thank you!'

The warmth of her smile and the delighted expression in her eyes almost made up to him for losing the argument.

'Just a word of advice,' he urged, but he knew she wasn't listening to a word he was saying. Impulsive as the devil and damned determined into the bargain. Who would have thought it?

He made one final plea to drive some sense into her head. This time he approached the matter from a different angle. 'At least take your aunt on the trip with you. You can afford the extra expense.'

The green eyes were incredulous. 'Take Aunt Edith on a trip halfway around the world? You just don't know her.' The smile that had so entranced him earlier in the interview flashed out, and he had to admit that it was worth waiting for. 'Honestly, she would never agree to that. She gets travel-sick even on a short journey. Oh, I'll ask her to come with me, but I know what the answer will be.'

It was no use. The solicitor bowed to the inevitable.

A short while later, with legal formalities completed, Sarah put the cheque he had given her into her bag and slipped the straps over her shoulder.

Rising from his chair, he saw her to the door. 'You'll let me know if you need my advice——'

'Oh, I'll need lots of that, but not about travelling out to New Zealand!'

The door closed on her laughing face.

Sarah and her aunt made their farewells as they stood together on the rain-swept platform of the local railway station. The cutting wind fluttered Sarah's woollen scarf round her shoulders and whipped deeper colour into the older woman's plump rosy cheeks.

'I'll write every week,' Sarah promised, 'and send you oodles of snapshots of the vineyard.'

Aunt Edith's blue eyes misted with tears, but her cheery smile got through. 'Just so long as you don't go falling in love with one of those husky New Zealand males—what do they call them? Kiwis?'

'Don't worry, I won't! I'll be back before you know it. It's only a holiday, and besides——' The hiss and roar of the approaching engine drowned out Sarah's words.

'Goodbye! Goodbye! Take care!' A warm hug, a parting kiss, and soon Sarah was leaning from the carriage window, waving back until the small feminine figure on the platform dwindled to a dot in the distance.

Sarah had planned her arrival at Gatwick Airport allowing time to spare before her departure, but she found that time dragged once the necessary formalities had been completed. At last, however, she was taking her seat in the great white Air New Zealand aircraft with its distinctive Maori motif of the *koru* emblazoned on the tail.

Presently safety belts were fastened, the engines roared into life and soon the plane was airborne. Sarah could scarcely contain her excitement. Farewell, grey wintry skies! Welcome, South Pacific sunshine!

'You're looking mighty pleased with yourself!' The masculine tones were tinged with amusement, and Sarah, turning to face her seat companion, had a quick impression of a thin, intense-looking man, probably in his early forties, with a lined face and jaded expression.

'Oh, I am! I am!' She smiled up at him. Somehow today she was in a mood for smiling at everyone she met.

Brushing back a lock of lank hair from his forehead, he said companionably, 'Hi! We've got a long haul ahead of us, so we may as well get acquainted. I'm Ewan and you're——?'

'Sarah.'

'Great to be heading back to good old New Zealand, isn't it?' He had a rapid way of speaking.

'Wonderful.' Her green eyes were a-sparkle. 'But it's not home to me. At least——' a secret smile played around her lips '—not yet.'

His sharp gaze took in her clear eyes still alight with excitement. 'What's the big attraction in Kiwi-land? It must be something a bit more than a tourist trip to make you look like that. If you ask me, I'd say you're off on the adventure of a lifetime and you just can't wait to get on with it! Your eyes are positively electric, and I don't flatter myself it's on my account.'

'I know, I can't help it,' she murmured ruefully. She glanced up at him animatedly. 'You'd never guess. I still can scarcely believe it. It's magic! I had this incredible news. It still seems like a dream.' Beneath his intent gaze the words tumbled from her lips. 'A legacy—quite a large sum of money and a house. What I'm most thrilled about, though, is a vineyard out in New Zealand. And all because of a man I scarcely know. He left everything to me... in his will.'

Her companion eyed her thoughtfully. 'There must be a bit more to the story than that?'

'In a way.' Sarah's eyes were shadowed.

'It's OK, you don't need to spell it out,' he said gently. 'So now you're on your way to claim your inheritance?'

'Oh, yes!' Her spirits rose with a rush. 'I'm going out there to spend the summer in the vineyard. I'm going to work there, find out everything I can about it. You know, the planting of the vines, harvesting, spraying, bottling——'

'Oh, I know all about wine,' he put in. 'Goes with my job.' He had a lop-sided, almost cynical grin, she thought. 'One of the useless scraps of information I pick up all the time about this and that. Usually it goes out of my head once the need for it has gone, but with wine it's different. It's the most fascinating subject I've come across in my line of duty.'

'Now I know,' she burst out triumphantly. 'You're a writer, a feature writer for a newspaper, something like that?'

He nodded. 'Journalism's my line. One of the perks of the job is that it gets me around the country. I'll look you up some time. New Zealand wines are big news overseas and I've got quite a few interviews lined up with wine-makers all over the country. We're sure to meet up somewhere between here and there.'

Ewan proved to be an interesting speaker, and his anecdotes of dangerous and attention-holding experiences in trouble spots in war-torn countries kept Sarah both spellbound and amused as the hours went by.

She fell asleep, and awoke to the sight of a flood of molten gold over the eastern horizon and knew that the journey was nearing its end. It wasn't long before the plane was dropping height and, leaning forward eagerly in her seat, she glimpsed vast sheep-dotted stretches of green far below.

At last she was rising to her feet and reaching up to the overhead rack for her modest travel bag, and soon she was joining the line of passengers who were making their way along the aisle.

Someone touched her shoulder and she swung around to face Ewan's crooked grin. 'Good luck with your vineyard! Be seeing you!'

'Bye!' She tossed him a smile. 'Be seeing you' was just a saying. It was unlikely they would ever meet again, even in a country of only three million where the sheep outnumbered the people. The next moment she had forgotten him.

She could scarcely contain her excitement as she moved down the airport steps and out into the translucent sunshine.

How glad she was now that she had decided to travel light and purchase any garments she might need in the warmth of a New Zealand summer. For, carrying only her shoulder-bag and nylon travel bag, she moved quickly through the Customs formalities and was one of the first of the passengers to leave the departure hall.

In the spacious, well-appointed toilets, with their gleaming basins and long mirrors, she washed hands and face in warm water. Then, zipping open her bag, she exchanged the dark woollen suit in which she had left London for a crisp white cotton T-shirt and a short skirt of sturdy blue denim. With a sense of relief she peeled off her tights and slipped her bare feet into blue trainers.

She creamed her face with moisturiser and added a touch of mascara to her lashes—all the make-up she needed on this balmy morning with its promise of rising temperatures later in the day. A swift brushing of her hair and she felt ready for anything. As she met her reflection in the long mirror she couldn't help feeling a glow of satisfaction. No doubt about it. She looked like a girl who was prepared to lend a hand wherever needed in the life that lay ahead rather than the new owner of Sunvalley Vineyard, fresh out from England.

CHAPTER TWO

OUTSIDE in the clear bright sunshine Sarah was immediately conscious of the clarity of the atmosphere. Colours were intensified and the air fresher. Then she seated herself in the airport bus waiting to transport passengers to the city.

It seemed to her to be a long time before passengers from the plane on which she had travelled boarded the vehicle. Ewan was not among them, but what did it matter? she thought idly. He meant no more to her than a chance acquaintance she would never meet again.

Sarah leaned from the window, the soft, warm breeze tossing her hair in a veil across her eyes as the bus left the main highway to pass through modern shopping centres with their shady verandas and eye-catching display windows.

A short time later she found herself taking in city workers who were moving along Auckland's main street. In the colourful multi-cultural city the men wore crisp cotton shirts, immaculate linen work-shorts, knee-length socks. The girls looked fresh and cool in brightly patterned frocks, their high heels tapping along the pavements. All at once Sarah was disconcertingly aware of her whiter-than-white skin.

The next minute she came in sight of the harbour, where the sea glittered and shone like a thousand crystals flung on a sheet of rippled blue silk. Ferries, overseas liners, cargo vessels were moored at the wharves, and on the street the impressive bronze figure of a cloaked Maori warrior gazed out over the waters of the harbour to the shadowy slopes of Rangitoto, an extinct volcano about which she had read in her travel folder.

She found a travel agency on the waterfront, and as she approached the counter a young male clerk who had been daydreaming at his desk got to his feet with alacrity.

'Good morning!' Sarah greeted him. 'I've just this morning arrived in this country from London, so——' her eyes were brilliant '—could you help me to find my way around?'

He looked at her incredulously, his appreciative gaze taking in her fresh young face and excited expression. 'You've only just got here, looking the way you do, after a twenty-seven-hour flight? Tell me, how do you do it?'

'Easy.' She gave a bubbling laugh of sheer happiness. 'I'm so thrilled to be here! Now, could you tell me how I can get to Waimarie? I'm going to Sunvalley Vineyard; do you know it?'

'Heard of it? Who hasn't? Their special red wine has collected no end of accolades this year, here and overseas. Not that I've sampled it, worse luck—it's right out of my price range—but good luck to them! It's great that New Zealand wines are making a name for themselves in world markets. Waimarie, you said? It's a bit off the beaten track, but there's a bus leaving from outside this office at three this afternoon.'

A shadow had fallen over her eager expression. 'Not until then? I was hoping——'

'No problem. There's a coach tour leaving here . . .' he consulted his wrist-watch '. . . in half an hour's time. It'll take you most of the way, but to get to the vineyard you'll have to cut along a road through the bush. So if you don't mind a bit of a hike——'

'*Mind*?' Her eyes were shining once again. 'I can't wait!'

'How about luggage? If you have to walk——'

'I've only got this.' She slipped the bag from her shoulder and laid it on the counter.

'You'll be right.' It was an expression with which she was to become familiar in the weeks ahead. He added, 'You'll have time to grab a coffee in the café next door. Have fun!'

She tossed him a laughing glance over her shoulder. 'It's my own fault if I don't. I mean, it's all waiting for me down there in Sunvalley!'

In the clean, attractive café Sarah was much too strung-up to be tempted by the array of luscious muffins and savouries arranged along glass counters. She sipped coffee from a pottery mug, then left to seat herself in the waiting tour coach.

She had a window-seat, and as the vehicle drew out into the city traffic she gazed out at the passing scenes where picturesque brick and stone buildings of an earlier era were dwarfed by soaring towers, the glass windows reflecting shimmering pictures of fragments of streets, trees growing in tubs near the pavements and glimpses of cloud and sky.

When they left the city behind they passed through districts where roadside entrances were lined with tall trees and a rough board nailed to a tree advertised fruit for sale—peaches, nectarines, melons, passion-fruit. Gradually the timber bungalows became further apart and they climbed bush-covered slopes where there seemed no sign of habitation beyond fleeting glimpses of a homestead set high on a hill-top, stockyards by the roadside far below, and always the shadowy blue of distant hills.

A long time later they reached a summit of a hill, and Sarah felt the cooling touch of the wind blowing blissfully on her hot face. Wood-smoke drifted from somewhere in a valley below and a bird's trilling notes sounded loud in the stillness.

The next minute she realised they were leaving the highway and swinging into a side-road, a rough metal pathway winding through densely growing native bush. As they went on the winding track led deeper into the bush, shadowy in the gullies, glinting with lighter green where umbrella-like fronds of softly waving pungas were bathed in sunshine. Here in the depths of the bush the heat was intense, and Sarah wiped the beads of perspiration from her dust-coated forehead.

At last they were sweeping down to a grassy clearing in filtered sunlight, and the driver brought the vehicle to a stop. He swung around, his gaze seeking Sarah. 'Your stop, Miss Smith.'

For a moment she took no notice, then the penny dropped. 'Smith'—the name on her passport and her baggage. She stared at him blankly. 'But I can't see any sign of a vineyard—or anything. Are you sure this is the place?'

'Not to worry.' His weathered face broke into a friendly grin. 'The vineyard is close by but out of sight. Just keep going along the track and you'll come to a bridge over a river. You'll hit the vineyard right beside it. You're nearly there!'

'But I thought I'd have a long walk to get there—— Oh!' Realisation came with a rush. 'But that means you've come ever so far out of your way just to drop me here.'

'A pleasure,' he assured her cheerfully. 'You'll be OK now on your own?'

'I'll be fine,' she smiled.

'Quite a place, Sunvalley,' he was saying. 'You'll like it. Good luck!'

As she went lightly down the high steps to the dust of the roadway a chorus of good wishes echoed around her. 'See you! Take care! Go easy on the *vino*. Have one on me! Goodbye! Goodbye! Good luck!'

A small figure set against the immensity of bush-clad hills, she stood watching and waving as the coach swung around, then moved away in a cloud of yellow dust in the direction of the main highway.

She straightened her shoulders and made her way along the dried grass at the edge of the narrow track. Here in this empty world there seemed nothing but the encroaching bush, the droning of bees and the pungent odour of crushed pennyroyal rising from the ground beneath her feet. All at once she caught sight of a weathered signpost nailed to a tree-trunk: 'Sunvalley Vineyard'. She rounded a bend in the track, then paused, spellbound, for below her were the vines. Row after row of branches twisted over wire fences with long avenues of grass between the rows. A rose-bush in full bloom marked the end of each row. It was very still in the valley. A haze lay over the surrounding hills, but the sun directly overhead burnished the vines in the sheltered valley where the grapes hung in clusters, rich and plump and purple and surely, she thought, all but ready for harvesting.

At last she tore her fascinated gaze aside and made her way along the winding path towards the imposing grey stone house at the top of the grassy slope.

Suddenly she came in sight of an old cottage almost hidden by encroaching spears of scarlet-flowered bougainvillaea and a gnarled grapevine spreading over the roof. Of course, she thought with a pang, this would be the original home of the European wine-maker who had brought his grape cuttings from his far-away homeland. It would have been Steven's home too before he built the big house on the rise he had intended for himself and his English bride.

She passed a swimming-pool shaded by overhanging hibiscus bushes, the fallen pink blossoms floating on the limpid, sun-warmed water. There were outbuildings not far from the house. Open garages held a car and a pick-up van and a tractor stood in the driveway.

Sarah went on to an area where a road branched off the main pathway and an arrow high on a board overhead pointed the way to 'Conference-Room' and 'Helipad'. Heavens, she thought in amazement, a helipad!

At last she reached a wide driveway leading to the sombre-looking stone house on the ridge above, and soon she was running lightly up the steps leading to an entrance porch. Sunshine streamed in at wide-open french windows and a black Labrador dog dozing on the mat got to his feet and wagged a friendly tail at the sight of her.

Sarah pressed a bell, catching the echo of chimes somewhere inside the house.

The next minute she found herself facing a woman with bare suntanned feet and wearing a vividly patterned sundress. The low-cut neckline of the frock revealed leathery brown shoulders, heavily spattered with freckles. Small, thin, sharp-featured, she regarded Sarah warily. 'Yes?' she queried.

'Oh, hello!' Sarah decided to ignore the woman's off-putting expression. Maybe living in this isolated area had made her become suspicious of strangers. 'You don't know me, but——' Her smile that had captivated the heart of the London lawyer lost a little of its lustre. 'My name's Sarah. I've heard all about the vineyard and I've come——'

'*You*!' The woman's gaze was taking in the Air New Zealand label on Sarah's travel bag. 'You're from England, aren't you?' Her face had flushed a dark, angry red and she was regarding Sarah with downright aversion.

'I've only just arrived this morning——'

'Oh, I know who you are! You're that awful girl from England!' The feminine tones rose high, out of control. 'Well, let me tell you something! You'll get no welcome here! Not while I'm in charge of the house! You'll have to find somewhere to stay.' She spat out the words vindictively. 'Maybe the farmhouse at the end of the road will take you in as a paying guest!'

Sarah moistened dry lips. 'But I thought——'

'You thought wrong, then, if you expected to stay here. Just go!'

'Good afternoon,' drawled a richly masculine voice, and Sarah spun around to face the dark-haired young man who had mounted the steps. At the same moment the small red-faced woman, who had been standing with one hand resting on the door-latch, turned and vanished inside the house.

'Nick's the name.' Relaxed and smiling, he eyed her with lazy interest. 'What's the problem? Anything I can sort out?'

'Oh, *yes*!' For a moment Sarah forgot everything else but her companion. Lean and muscular, with softly waving dark hair, and deep smile-lines, male dimples, running down each side of well-shaped lips, the stranger was heart-stoppingly attractive in a relaxed, sun-bronzed sort of way.

The thoughts raced wildly through her mind. He projected an aura of rugged vitality and masculine charisma that was positively devastating. Why, she could almost feel it! She gave herself a mental shake and jerked herself back to sanity. All this clear bright sunshine must be going to her head. Maybe if she didn't look directly into those thickly lashed dark eyes she would be more in control of her runaway senses.

'What was it you wanted?' The resonant tones cut across the confusion of her responses. She hesitated, the carefully prepared speeches she had devised for this situation gone from her mind. Blame it on the shock of the strange woman's reaction to my arrival there, Sarah thought. All at once she was finding it difficult to make known her identity to the man at her side.

'It's just——' She heard her own voice, determinedly cheerful. 'I wonder if I could have a word with the manager here? That is——' the glint of amusement in his alive-looking dark eyes was unnerving, but she struggled on '—if he's around just now?'

'Sure is.' She caught the flash of strong white teeth in a deeply suntanned face. 'You're having a word with him right now!'

Sarah's eyes widened in surprise. 'You mean,' she murmured incredulously, 'that you're the boss of Sunvalley?'

'Let's just say——' there was an ironic inflexion in the richly masculine tones '—that I'm keeping the show on the road—for the moment.'

'But...' the words were out before she could stop to think '...I thought you were one of the workers here. You know, someone who looks after the vines.' The thought came unbidden that if he could look so wildly attractive in work-stained T-shirt and tattered denim shorts—— She thrust the truant imaginings aside.

'Right again.' At the quizzical note in his voice she glanced up, and their glances meshed and held. All at once she was piercingly aware of him. Her pulses leaped and for a crazy moment the sunlight seemed to shimmer and dance around her. She couldn't seem to tear her glance away from those magnetic dark eyes. At last she wrenched her gaze aside.

'What was it you wanted to see me about?' The rich, drawling tones seemed to come from a distance.

'Well, actually——' She tried to pull her thoughts together. Somehow she was finding it awfully difficult to make known her identity to this stranger. The angry little woman had not reappeared, so at least that was something to be thankful for. At last she heard her own voice, sounding light and carefree—well, almost. 'My name's Sarah and I've come out from England. I——'

'Sarah!' In an instant all the light-hearted expression had fled from his features. The line of his jaw was taut and his eyes darkened formidably. All at once the atmosphere was tense with emotion and she knew that something was dreadfully wrong.

'Sarah Sinclair,' she said quickly. Let him make what he liked out of that!

He shot her a probing glance. 'Did you say—Sinclair?'

'That's me,' she agreed cheerfully, determined not to allow herself to be intimidated by this daunting stranger.

Suddenly his face cleared and the dark eyes that had been like chips of black ice a few moments ago were glinting and full of light. 'Guess I got my wires crossed!' His sudden smile was heartwarming. 'I mistook you for another girl.'

Sarah was silent, pushing the thick brown hair behind her ears in a nervous gesture as the thoughts rushed chaotically through her mind. One thing was for sure. She wouldn't be staying here as she had planned, not in view of the housekeeper's angry reaction to her sudden appearance. It was odd, though, that her name didn't seem to ring any bell in the mind of the boss. But of course! Realisation came with a rush. How could it, when the name of the girl who had inherited the vineyard, the name that appeared on Steven's will as well as her own current passport, was Sarah no-nonsense Smith? *He didn't know*. She wondered what he would say if she came right out with it and announced, 'I am that other girl!'

'Now I get it.' An expression of relief took the place of his puzzled look. The deep, relaxed tones went on, 'You've come in answer to the job I advertised in the local rag a week or two ago, offering casual work in the vineyard?'

Too taken aback to think clearly, Sarah hesitated. Evidently he had taken her silence for assent, she thought the next minute, wrenching her mind back to his tones.

'I was hoping someone would show up to help out. I'm harvesting the grapes almost right away and my usual team of local women who come to the vineyard for the picking each year is a bit depleted. The ad didn't give any particulars, but what I'm looking for is a girl who can make herself useful around the place, picking grapes, bottling, labelling, able to do a stint in the bottle store and attend to mail orders—maybe even lend a hand in the reception-room when the tour buses drive in for a barbecue meal or a party of wine buffs drop in for a tour around the winery.

'Actually,' he ran on, 'I'd given up expecting any replies to my ad. But at least someone must have read it. You must be the exception. The farmers' daughters around the district move to the city to find work once they've finished with high school. Anyone from out of the district who comes here can't take the isolation, and you can't blame them. But of course——' his eyes, half closed against the sun-glare, rested on her pale face '—you're not a local girl.'

The thought ran through her distraught mind that he too had not missed the significance of her travel bag. If only he didn't catch sight of her name on the Air New Zealand label.

His next words, however, reassured her on that point. 'Tell me, how long have you been in this part of the world?'

Careful. Don't let him know you have only just arrived here. 'Not long,' she told him.

'Just as I thought.' She moved uneasily beneath his appraising glance. 'So you didn't come in answer to my ad?'

'No.' She had an uneasy suspicion that he was a man who wouldn't miss anything, especially anything you wished to keep secret from him. His lazy, drawling voice had deceived her.

'You're just out from England, aren't you?' he added.

What was the use of hiding the truth? 'I arrived here this morning!' Sarah's voice was bright with challenge, but once again she couldn't sustain the impact of his mocking dark glance. 'Why?' she demanded. 'Does it matter?'

'Not to me.' A half-smile touched his lips. 'But it shows.'

'What do you mean?' She raised questioning eyes to his amused grin.

There was a glint of male interest in his gaze. 'You don't come across many girls looking the way you do in this part of the world. That honey-and-cream complexion——'

'Me?' she said in disbelief, all too aware of her forehead sticky with perspiration, dust-smeared garments, hair blown every which way in the breeze blowing in at the open window of the coach. And yet he really seemed to mean it. A simple compliment, so why did her senses go flying into confusion? She could feel the pink colour creeping up her cheeks. For some reason she couldn't fathom this stranger was having a disturbing effect on her emotions.

'How did you find your way down here?' he asked. Thankful that his query had no concern with her reason for her seeking out the vineyard, she could answer truthfully. 'On a tour bus from Auckland. It was a fantastic trip through the bush.'

Suddenly his expression hardened. 'So long as you didn't try hitch-hiking through the country. I wouldn't advise it.'

Sarah felt a flash of irritation. Who did he think he was, for heaven's sake? Telling her what she could and could not do when he didn't even know her? 'I can look after myself,' she said stiffly.

The next moment her thoughts reverted to her own problem. The memory of the sudden hardening of his expression when he had mistaken her for that other Sarah niggled in her mind. Worriedly she twisted a lock of hair round and round her finger. Oh, no doubt he was in need of a worker in the vineyard, but he didn't want Sarah Smith at Sunvalley, any more than did his housekeeper.

'I've had the odd boy and girl from overseas call in here other summers,' he was saying, 'from England, Europe, whatever. They were making their way through the country, picking up casual work as they went along, packing kiwi-fruit, harvesting grapes in the vineyards or doing a stint of apple- and peach-picking in the orchards. Usually they're students seeing the country and keeping their travel expenses going at the same time. I guess that goes for you too? You're here on a working holiday, looking for work in the vineyard?'

Looking for work in the vineyard? Well, that was one way of putting it. 'Yes, yes, I am!' There was no need to disguise the eagerness of her tone.

All the time, however, her thoughts were rioting in confusion. He was offering her an escape route. She still had a chance to stay here and fulfil her longing to get to know the workaday life of this vineyard. Could she carry off the deception? And suppose she was to be found out? From nowhere came the thought, If only the boss weren't so devastatingly attractive. If only I didn't have to deceive him. All at once she had a sick feeling in her stomach. What if he was to discover that she was a liar and a cheat? Worse, he might even suspect her of sneakily coming to Sunvalley under another name in order to check on the integrity of the manager of her far-away property.

It would only be for the summer, whispered the tiny voice of temptation. Then I'll go back to England and no one here will ever know.

And I'll never see him again. Now where had that absurd thought come from? she chided herself the next moment. She must indeed be suffering from a touch of the hot, unfamiliar sun!

'Tell me,' the drawling tones cut across her frantic musing, 'you've no plans for taking off for somewhere else in a week or so?'

She shook her head. No plans? If he only knew!

'I don't know about you, Sarah.' She shifted uneasily beneath his considering gaze. 'As I said, I'm harvesting the grapes any day now and I'm one short of my usual team of local women who come to help me out in the picking season.' He shot her one of the probing looks she was beginning to dread. 'Have you any idea of what you're taking on? Hours of back-breaking slog out there in the hot sun? You don't look all that—muscular, shall I say?' His assessing gaze flickered over the pale translucence of her skin, moved to her bare ankles, all but indistinguishable from the snowy leather of her sandals.

Beneath his scrutiny she felt a foolish tinge of colour in her cheeks. 'But I'm ever so strong,' she assured him spiritedly. 'You'd be surprised, honestly!'

His only comment was a sceptical lift of thickly marked black eyebrows. 'Ever done any outdoor work?'

'No,' she admitted, 'but I'm used to office work. I've done that for years.'

'And that's all?' His offhand tone gave nothing away, and she had a dreadful feeling that he had no intention of putting her on his payroll.

'Nothing else in the way of experience?' His cool, impassive tones sparked her to sudden defiance. She put on her brightest smile, or the best she could manage in the circumstances, and threw it over to fate. 'I play the guitar,' she told him recklessly, and added for good measure, 'and sing a bit.'

'You do?' To her amazement he was regarding her with sudden attention.

'Oh, not professionally,' she said. 'I just entertain for friends, office parties, that sort of thing.'

'Terrific!' His dark eyes were alight with interest. 'Tell me, what sort of music do you put on?'

She shrugged lightly. 'Just what anyone wants. Country music, ballads, folk-songs, anything with a swing to it.'

'That's great!' He still had that excited look about him.

Sarah's eyes held a puzzled expression. 'But I don't see—'

'Look over there,' he ordered.

'Where?' She followed his gesture towards what appeared to her to be a glasshouse, not far from the house.

'No, it's not just a glasshouse. It's a reception-room-cum-conference-room. Seats about two hundred people. Wine-makers come for meetings and tour buses bring groups looking for a barbecue lunch out in the wine country with an atmosphere and wine thrown in.'

Sarah tried to concentrate on his vibrant tones. 'Believe me, it's the devil of a job to find entertainers who are willing to come way out here for a single engagement, especially at short notice. Could be,' he was saying jubilantly, 'you're just the one I'm looking for!'

'Oh, my goodness!' She flung a hand to her mouth. 'I didn't bring my guitar with me.'

'Not to worry.' He brushed the matter aside with a wave of a well-shaped bronzed hand. 'That's no problem. Thing is, the job's yours if you want it.' His enthusiastic tones ran on, 'There's accommodation provided on the property—an old cottage, but it's well kept up and comfortable. I pay a bit over award rates and days off will be open to arrangement to suit us both. Depends a lot on the weather in this game. We'll play it by ear, shall we? Don't forget, if you have any problems come to me and I'll sort things out.' His smile, she thought once again, was really something. 'Care to give it a go?'

She couldn't believe her luck. 'Why not?'

'Terrific!' He took her hand in his firm grasp and once again she felt a stirring of her pulses. 'By the way, Juravich is my name, but Nick's near enough.'

Juravich. Steven's name. Sarah's hand went limp as she faced the moment of truth. He was no doubt a relative of the other man and could even be the rightful inheritor of the vineyard.

'Are you all right, Sarah?' She became aware of his concerned glance searching her face. 'You're looking very white all of a sudden. What's wrong?'

'Nothing, nothing.' She shook back the thick hair from her damp forehead in an attempt to dispel the mists that threatened to engulf her senses. 'I'm fine.' She forced a smile. 'It's just the heat.'

'My fault——' his eyes were dark with contrition '—for keeping you standing out here in the hot sun all this time. Come along inside and I'll get you a cool drink while I put you in the picture all about life, Sunvalley style. The working life, that is.'

He stood back and, scarcely aware of her movements, Sarah went through the opening of the french doors and into an adjoining room. It was too late now to confess her subterfuge. She was committed. All she could do was ride it out and hope for the best.

Striving to gather her wits together, she said, 'But you're in charge. Surely——'

'Makes no difference around here.'

But it made all the difference in the world to her, she thought. A winery manager with whom she would have little personal contact in the course of her day-to-day duties was one thing. Working alongside Nick Juravich with his male attraction, his aura of power and authority, was something else again.

'Take a seat.' She dropped down to a cane lounger with its colourful upholstered cushions. 'And I'll have a word with Kate, get her to rustle up something to eat. You must be ready for it after that long drive.'

He left the room to return in a few minutes. 'What would you like to drink? Wine cooler, orange or pineapple juice, a sherry——?'

'A wine cooler will be fine,' she told him.

'Kate's feeling a bit embarrassed,' he apologised. 'She'll be along soon, but right now she wants me to tell you she thought you were someone else—another Sarah. Just a misunderstanding.'

He handed her a crystal goblet and she sipped the drink, chilled and delicious with its flavour of mango.

A little later Kate entered the room, a plate of sandwiches in her hand.

'Hey, you two don't know each other yet,' Nick said easily. 'Kate, Sarah Sinclair. Sarah's going to stay for a while and help out with the harvesting and other jobs around the place.'

'Hello, Kate.' The genuine friendliness of Sarah's smile must have got through to the housekeeper, for, holding the plate of sandwiches towards Sarah, she muttered half under her breath, 'Sorry about—you know—what I said.' Sarah could barely catch the low words. 'It was all a mistake... now that Nick has explained——'

'Don't give it a thought,' Sarah said, relieved to find that Kate, for all her fly-away temper tantrum, bore her no ill will.

A little later when Kate had left them Nick stood looking down at Sarah. 'Right, Sarah, your working day starts tomorrow—seven a.m., and I'm warning you it'll be mighty hot out there among the vines. You've got to be tough to take the picking—backache, wasps and all!'

She sipped the delicious fruit-flavoured cooler. 'I don't mind. I don't mind *anything* if I can stay here for the summer——' She broke off in confusion, aghast at the emotional intensity betrayed in her tone. Pulling her thoughts together, she rushed on, 'So you run the vineyard on your own?'

He stared down into his empty glass. 'Nowadays I do. It's more or less a temporary arrangement.' Before she could ask any further questions he said, 'What part of England do you come from? I can't pick up any particular accent.'

'Oh, that's because I come from London.' It was true in a way, for hadn't she once lived there? 'Have you ever been to London?'

'No, but Steven had a trip overseas. He picked up all sorts of gen about wine-making from the vineyards in Europe he went to see.'

'Steven?' She held her breath.

'The previous owner. He and I were partners,' he said curtly.

She thought wildly, Now is the time for me to confess the truth about my visit here. But if I do I'll miss this incredible chance fate has handed me to stay on here, be a part of it all, belonging.

His cool, businesslike tones seemed to tune in on her thoughts. 'You're happy about the harvesting work, then?' All at once he was very much her employer. 'A hat's a must if you're going to avoid a dose of sunburn or worse.' For a moment his impassive tones softened. 'Better protect that fair skin of yours any way you can, and that includes sun-block.' He shot her a commanding glance. 'You've got sun-block cream with you? And you'll do as I say?'

She nodded in agreement, but she meant having the cream in her travel bag, not applying it. Really, of all the domineering employers!

'What else?' She raised her eyes to his and once again found herself trapped in the impact of his gaze. For a moment nothing else in the world existed for her but this compelling, daunting stranger. With an effort she broke the spell, heard her own voice saying, 'What would I need to do? I'm used to office work, and you mentioned mail orders——'

'They're way behind, so you'll have lots to catch up on. How about shop work? Ever done any selling?'

'No, but I could,' she assured him.

'There's not too much involved in that line—it's mostly mail order—but I need someone to help out in the bottle store, mainly when tour buses pull in or a coach drives in with a party of wine-buffs. There's always the odd customer or two who thinks the rough road to Sunvalley is worth the wine.' For a second a look of pride crossed his face. No doubt he had good reason for pride in his wine-making, she thought.

CHAPTER THREE

'RIGHT,' Nick said, 'that about wraps it up,' and, realising that the interview was at an end, Sarah got to her feet.

'If you're ready,' Nick offered, 'I'll take you for a tour around the place, show you the cottage where you'll be putting up—— Hey, let me take that!' He made a move towards her travel bag lying on the floor between them, but in a flash Sarah was kneeling beside it, ripping off the tell-tale name label with trembling fingers.

'I just wanted a handkerchief,' she mumbled.

They were moving down the steps when suddenly Sarah stood still, as the silence was broken by rapid blasts of sharp staccato sounds. 'Listen.' She turned to him, wide-eyed. 'Someone's shooting, and quite near here!'

He grinned. 'Not to worry. It's just the scare machine doing its job. It goes off at intervals to frighten away the birds. Not that they take much notice of it once they get used to the sound. That's why I've put nets over the vines this year. It's too close to harvesting time to lose the grapes now.'

When they reached ground level he led her down more steps, then flung open the great wooden doors. In contrast with the brilliant sunshine outside, the cellar was cool with its wet concrete floors, weathered timber casks and great steel vats. 'Later on,' Nick told her, 'the grapes are strained into small silver vats, stainless steel ones taken from outmoded models of milk tankers.'

They moved on to the stacks of boxes filled with bottles: 'Reds'. 'It all takes time,' Nick said. 'A year for planting, two for bottling, three for maturing.'

Presently they were once more out in the daylight, strolling over the dried grassy slope leading towards the rows of vines below.

'The cellars under the house,' he explained, 'are in line with the European wine-making philosophy.' His face was alight with enthusiasm. 'And I'm all for it! The wine-maker lives above the winery and controls everything, from the growing and harvesting of the grapes to labelling and marketing the wine. Sure it's time-consuming and labour-intensive, but what the heck! It means the winery is your life, and that's the way I like it.'

His deep tones glowed with interest, and Sarah had a feeling that, engrossed in the passion for his work, he had forgotten all about her. She wrenched her mind back to his voice. 'The old boy who started the vineyard came from Dalmatia with no money and a lot of hopes. He began his new life in New Zealand by living in a tent, grubbing kauri gum out of the ground way up north. When he fulfilled his dream of buying land here and starting a vineyard with vines he'd brought with him from his home country, he was determined this wasn't going to be an ordinary vineyard, not just a commercial thing. Steven, my partner, carried on the tradition. Working with him for so long, I guess a lot of his ideas rubbed off on to me. He wanted Sunvalley to be a specialist-style winery.' He paused, looking unseeingly over the vines in the valley below. 'Producing too many varieties only confuses the grower's aims and ambitions, detracts from the overall quality of the wine. I'd rather produce one line perfectly than ten lines only moderately well.' He's utterly dedicated to living and working in this vineyard, Sarah thought in dismay. It was an effort to concentrate on his resonant tones. 'Here we take care of every aspect of production from growing and harvesting the grapes to labelling and marketing the wine. Our winemaking venture was never a commercial thing. But it's worth building a lifestyle around.'

A lifestyle! In an effort to dispel the feelings of guilt and uneasiness his words had aroused in her she gestured towards the rose-bushes in full bloom, each bush planted at the head of a row of vines. 'Tell me, are the rose-bushes a European custom too in vineyards?' she asked.

He followed her gaze. 'You've guessed it. *Larose* is actually the old French spelling. The rose for me is the ultimate flower, the symbol of perfection.'

'Really?' She threw him a laughing glance. 'I wouldn't have thought you'd be so romantic as to plant roses among the grapes——'

'It's functional.' His dismissive tone chilled her. 'If any disease attacks the grapes it'll show up first on the rose-bush.'

'Oh!' She was glad that at that moment the black Labrador came to join them. Nick bent to pat the dog's head. 'This is Sam,' he told Sarah, and they moved towards the vines running up the slopes.

For something to say, Sarah murmured, 'It looks so tidy, all those rows of vines running up the slopes of the hill.'

'They're aligned north-south to maximise sun exposure,' Nick explained.

'And the buildings?' She turned to gaze back to the sheds and outbuildings a short distance from the house. 'I thought they'd be where the wine was made and stored.'

'Not at Sunvalley. When Steven built the house he wanted to follow the family lifestyle of the wine-maker, living above the winery and controlling everything closely interconnected with the family.' All at once his eyes darkened. 'Too bad that things didn't work out that way for him. Not like his grandfather, who started it all. The old boy really tamed the wilderness here, cleared away gorse and blackberry, planted the macrocarpa trees as a shelterbelt from the prevailing winds. You know something, Sarah? The family lifestyle has a lot going for it. The old boy and his family worked on the land non-stop for most of their lives, but they won out in the end.'

She eyed him in some surprise. 'You mean his wife and his sons and daughters worked here together all their lives?'

'Why not?' His smooth tone was maddening.

She pulled a face. 'It doesn't sound much fun for his wife——'

'But she was in agreement. She liked nothing better than husband and wife working side by side, and later on their children too. That's the way she wanted it.'

'I bet he never asked the girl he was marrying,' she flung at him, 'if she wanted to live that way, having to work flat out for ever and ever!'

His dark eyes mocked her. 'Why should he ask her? He knew nothing would give her more enjoyment, a satisfaction that would last for all her life. Even today——'

'Today!' Oh, he made her so angry! Could it be the shock and frustrations of the day that made her feel so furious with him? He was mocking her, she was certain of it. You only had to catch the satirical gleam in his eyes. She said incredulously, 'You'll never find a girl like that these days. They're an endangered species! Or hadn't you noticed?'

'Oh, I wouldn't say that,' came the rich, drawling tones. 'For two people who love each other to want to work together——'

Sarah refused to meet his mocking gaze. 'You'll never find this girl you're so enthusiastic about. Anyway, what girl would want to be like that—someone who's so meek and mild that she's way back in Victorian times, passionately interested in wine production, does everything she's told and will work to please you day and night?' Vindictively she added, 'All for no wages!'

'What are wages——' the black eyebrows rose '—when she's a partner in a wonderful lifestyle with equal shares of fun and profits?'

She said darkly, 'If there is any fun—or profits.' Why was she feeling so worked up about this mythical female anyway? 'Don't tell me,' she taunted, 'that you've got her picked out already?'

His eyes were bright and intent. 'I'm working on it.' She threw him a disbelieving look, and all at once his tone was deceptively soft. 'In the wine countries of the Adriatic there's a saying that to achieve perfection everything that's done with wine should be done with love.'

She threw him a suspicious glance, but his enigmatic expression gave nothing away. Unbidden, a thought crossed her mind. Had fate decreed that her sister Kathy should come out to New Zealand and marry her Steven, would she have been content to work alongside him in the vineyard? She had been deeply in love with him. Sarah shied away from the answer.

'It's true.' Something in Nick's low accents was oddly disturbing and she heard herself rushing into speech. 'Let's go down to the valley and take a closer look at the vines, shall we?'

'Come on, then!' Together they ran down the grassy hillside, to come to a breathless stop beside the evenly spaced rows of vines with their long avenues of grassy strips dividing the rows. Tiny birds with fan-like tails zigzagged their fluttering way above the nets and small blue moths hovered in the air. In the shelter of the vines the heat was oppressive. Sarah could feel tendrils of hair clinging to her flushed, damp forehead. But the grapes hung in purple perfection in cluster after cluster, and for a few blissful moments she forgot everything else, even Nick, in the enjoyment of her surroundings.

'You'll see plenty of this tomorrow,' Nick told her. 'Next stop the glasshouse!'

Presently he was showing her into a long reception-room where the walls were lined with windows and grapes hung in clusters from vines trained over the ceiling. Small tables and chairs were scattered along the walls and a well-stocked bar ran along the end of the room.

'Now for the office,' Nick told her as they moved out into the sunshine. 'It's fairly basic.' In a swift glance around her Sarah took in a worn desk piled high with account books, order books, files and correspondence. There was an electric typewriter and a filing cabinet. On the walls were pinned newspaper clippings featuring presentations of wine awards as well as framed certificates. She noticed that one certificate was recent and named Sunvalley Red as the top New Zealand export wine of the year. Empty crates and boxes littered the floor.

Nick's drawling tones broke into her thoughts. 'The typewriter's OK for you?'

'Oh, yes, it's fine.' Privately she was thinking that the grimy windows could well do with a wash and the litter of papers piled haphazardly over the desk would be easier dealt with if arranged in some sort of order.

'That's about it,' Nick was saying. 'Come and see the cottage.'

Sarah's steps quickened as they neared the small stone building, the entrance all but hidden in encroaching greenery. A gnarled grapevine framed the roof and bougainvillaea rioted in a tide of brilliant magenta blossoms over the porch.

'On the islands of the Adriatic, houses are built of brick or stone—it's traditional.' She caught a flash of strong white teeth in Nick's sun-bronzed face. 'They have a saying in their country, "What we Yugoslavs do, we do well."'

'And you?' Because the answer to her question meant so much to her she had difficulty in schooling her voice to a light, carefree note. 'Are you of that nationality too?'

'Not so you'd notice it.' His voice was careless. 'It's way back, the connection.'

'How far—back?' Her words came from a dry throat, but he didn't seem to notice the rasp in her voice.

He shrugged broad shoulders. 'Steven's the one who was a direct descendant of the original owner of the vineyard. I happen to be a distant relative of his brother, who came out to New Zealand in the early days and planted his own vineyard.' He grinned. 'Guess I inherited the name along with the wine-making instinct. Old Ivan did well with his wine-making in the end.' His lively glance challenged her. 'He had the good sense to marry an English girl who'd only just stepped off the sailing ship that brought her out to New Zealand—— Am I boring you?'

'No, no, you're not. It's all so different, a new world to me.' His glinting gaze was difficult to meet and to Sarah's chagrin she could feel the pink colour rising in her cheeks. What was it about this stranger that could so disturb her? His simplest remark seemed to have the power to throw her into a state of confusion. 'You were saying——?' Thank heaven her voice sounded normal enough.

'About the English girl?' This time she avoided his mocking look. 'Mind you——' his drawling tones changed her moment of confusion to a sharp annoyance '—he was lucky to have found her before some other guy snapped her up. He badly needed a wife to give him a hand in his vineyard, and in those pioneering days in the new country unmarried girls were as scarce as hen's teeth.'

Sarah flung him an exasperated glance. 'They'd have been scarcer still if they'd known what they were letting themselves in for. He didn't give the girl a chance to meet anyone else!' Before he could continue to amuse himself at her expense she ran on crisply, 'Let's go inside, shall we? I can't wait to see it.'

'Why not?' He flung open the door, and she tried to adjust her vision in the sudden dim light. The next moment Nick strode across the room to pull aside the curtains and fling open the windows, letting in the breeze spiced with the tang of the nearby bush.

'Nice,' Sarah murmured, taking in the beamed ceiling and white plastered walls. Her gaze moved to a well-worn couch, a dresser stacked with racks of willow-patterned china and a kauri table with sturdy chairs.

'The kitchen's this way.' Nick pulled aside a dividing curtain and she saw with some surprise that the spotlessly clean room held an electric range as well as a combined refrigerator and deep-freeze cabinet.

Nick threw open a cupboard door, revealing stocks of tea, sugar, powdered milk, packets of biscuits, coffee, Marmite and honey. 'There's swags of frozen stuff in the deep-freeze up at the house. Just let Kate know if you need anything; she's used to folk putting up here in the picking season.'

A door in the living-room led to a bedroom, where twin beds were covered in crocheted lace spreads and flimsy nylon curtains billowed out in the breeze as Nick flung open the windows. There was a bathroom complete with hot and cold shower, a toilet and, unexpectedly, an automatic washing-machine.

Back in the living-room his deep tones reached her. 'Reckon you've got everything you want here?'

At last her smile was for real and she could answer truthfully. 'Oh, yes, it's comfortable.'

'Right! Seven o'clock in the morning, sun-block and all—— Don't forget!'

'I won't!' Sarah's lips were set in a mutinous line and once again she meant about the picking and not, most definitely not, about the sun-block!

She stared resentfully after the tall masculine figure who was striding back along the path, the black Labrador at his heels. Of all the autocratic, interfering males she had ever encountered! Of course he was her boss while she was here and she was agreeable to go along with his instructions regarding her duties. But of all the nerve! Giving her orders concerning personal matters that were entirely her own affair. Sun-block indeed! On the contrary, she *wanted* to acquire a suntan, a deep honey-gold shade preferably, and in the shortest possible time. Swathing herself in covering clothing and smothering herself in sun-block cream was the last thing she wanted to do. Unconsciously Sarah lifted her chin. She would certainly demonstrate to Nick tomorrow morning that she hadn't the slightest intention of following his unasked-for advice!

The long summer twilight was fading when Sarah answered a knock on the door to find Kate standing outside, a pile of towels in her arms.

'Come in.' Sarah bent to switch off her transistor radio.

'You'll be needing these.' Kate avoided Sarah's gaze. 'I'll pop them in the cupboard.'

'Thank you,' smiled Sarah.

'It wasn't just because of the towels I came to see you.' The muffled tones came from the direction of the linen cupboard in a corner of the room. 'I feel badly about this morning, letting fly at you like that! I wanted to explain, to tell you——'

'Think nothing of it.' Sarah was glad of the deepening shadows in the room that hid her expression. 'There's no need——'

Kate, however, refused to be put off. 'Oh, but there is! I just want you to know, I jumped to conclusions.

When you said your name was Sarah and you'd come from England, I really thought it was *her*.' All at once Kate's tones were sharp and vindictive. 'I wouldn't put it past her to land here on the doorstep without a word of warning! I wouldn't put anything past that one. She——'

'Excuse me,' Sarah broke in desperately, 'would you care for a coffee?'

Kate waved the suggestion aside. 'No, thanks. Well, as I was saying, it all happened ages ago. Steven, my nephew, owned the vineyard then, and when he'd been at Sunvalley for some years he decided to take a trip to Europe and pick up ideas about improving his vineyard here. On the way home he stayed for a few weeks in London, and that's where he met the English girl—Kathy was her name. In no time at all they were engaged to be married.' Her thin lips tightened. 'Oh, she knew what she was about, that one, when she persuaded him to get engaged to her only three weeks after they met.'

Sarah opened her lips to protest, then closed them again. Through the tumult of her thoughts she tried to focus her mind on the merciless feminine tones. 'Steven was head over heels in love, or thought he was. When he got back here he was full of plans for the future, determined to have a new house built and ready for living in when his Kathy arrived in the country to marry him. He could talk of nothing but her.' All at once a little of the venom died out of the angry tones. 'That's why he was so hard hit when he got the news that she'd been killed in a road accident on the way to the airport.'

Sarah could find no words, but it didn't matter, she decided the next moment, for Kate was running on, her eyes hard and unforgiving, 'Anyway, this Kathy had a young sister—Sarah. There's a photo of her around the place somewhere, taken with Steven and her sister—a skinny-looking kid with her hair tied back in a pony-tail. Trust her to push herself into the picture with the other two! She was so cunning, that kid, always buttering him up——'

'How do you mean,' Sarah asked sharply, cutting into the rapid flow of words, 'buttering him up?'

'Oh, you know, she kept writing letters to him for the first year or so after the accident, and after that she sent him a Christmas card for quite a few years, prodding his memory, keeping herself in with him.'

Sarah couldn't have spoken for the choking sensation in her throat. Kate was speaking fast and furiously. What was she saying now? Something about the will? 'And then when he died suddenly the most awful thing happened! It seems that Steven's will had been drawn up with the lawyers in London all these years earlier, leaving everything he owned to the girl he meant to marry and, failing her being alive, the estate, money, everything he possessed passed to her nearest relative. All of it left to *her*—a child he'd only known for a short time all those years ago! She'll be grown up by now, and I bet she's as wily and devious as they come. I expect her sister told her all about the will at the time it was drawn up. And she'd never forget about it. It would be her big chance. It makes me so *mad*,' Kate burst out angrily, 'to think that it's all hers! Just because Steven had never made a new will.'

'Nick——?' Sarah couldn't voice the fear in her mind, but fortunately Kate didn't appear to notice the lurch in her voice.

'Nick's a lot younger than Steven. He'd always wanted to work with the vines, and when Steven got back from his overseas trip he took Nick in with him here, trained him in all the workings of wine-making from planting the vines to bottling the wine. They were equal partners in Sunvalley—well, not legally, they never got around to having things tied up with the lawyer, but it was always understood that if anything happened to Steven Nick would take over full ownership. And now...' Her voice trailed away into a heavy silence.

Sarah asked a question that was tugging at her mind. 'Nick was a relative of Steven, then?' Could that be her own voice, sounding so thick and strange?

Kate hesitated. 'In a way. He was a distant cousin, something like that. Funny to think he has so little Yugoslav blood in his veins, yet all the expertise and love of wine-making seems to have come out in him. Nick was the nearest thing to a relative that Steven possessed—he thought the world of him. It was the most terrible shock when Steven died suddenly. Everyone just took it for granted that Nick would take over Sunvalley as owner, and now...that's what makes it all so dreadful. Sunvalley is different from wineries in other parts of the country. It's so much smaller than others, for one thing, and Nick—well, Sunvalley isn't just a vineyard to him, it's his whole life. So you do see——' she sent Sarah a shamefaced glance from beneath her lashes '—that's why when you came here this morning...you do understand?'

'Don't worry.' Sarah tried to make her voice light and friendly. 'I've forgotten all about it already.' And she thought with a sick sense of foreboding, If only I could.

* * *

At first, awakening after a white night spent tossing and turning endlessly, Sarah was surprised to find herself in unfamiliar surroundings. Then realisation came with a rush. A swift glance towards the bedroom clock on a table at her side told her that in her agitated state of mind last evening she had neglected to set her alarm. But she could still get to the vines in time! Still in pyjamas, she opened a carton of yoghurt, toasted a slice of bread and mixed a mug of instant coffee. Then swiftly she rifled through her meagre wardrobe, determined to demonstrate her defiance of Nick's high-handed orders. She settled for a yellow halter-top and matching shorts. There! That should prove a point to Nick, who considered himself to be such an authority on feminine clothing and skin care. Her soft lips firmed. But she would show him!

Soon she was moving along the winding, overgrown pathway to join the group of women who were gathered near the vines while Nick handed out blue plastic bins.

As she neared the group she was met by welcoming smiles, and she smiled and waved in return. 'This is Sarah,' Nick told the others shortly.

'Hi, Sarah! Glad to meet you! Join the club!' Cheerful warm greetings echoed around her, then the pickers moved away to start their work at the beginning of the long rows of vines.

Nick stood alone and he looked anything but warm and welcoming, Sarah thought, for there was no mistaking the tight line of his lips or the anger that smouldered in his dark eyes.

Deliberately she took her time as she strolled over the dew-wet grass to join him. She forced a smile. 'Not late, am I?'

'You're not late.' His cold stare was forbidding.

'Oh, I thought maybe I was.' She slanted him a glance from under her lashes and decided to take the initiative. 'You look so disapproving.'

The expression in his dark eyes was formidable. 'I *am* disapproving. And don't pretend you don't know what I'm on about!' His disparaging glance swept over her. 'All the wrong clothing for a day's picking out in the hot sun—and no sun-block!'

'That's right,' she agreed crisply. 'No sun-block.'

Suddenly his voice was cold steel. 'Why didn't you do as I told you? Protect yourself from the sun?'

Raising her small chin, Sarah said cheekily, 'I don't *have* to do what you tell me to!'

'No?' His drawling tones were loaded with menace.

Despite her resolution not to allow herself to be rattled by him, the force of his personality, his aura of power and authority of which she had been conscious from their first moment of meeting struck her anew. Reluctantly she reminded herself that he was her employer in the vineyard, and rather spoiled her defiant statement by adding, 'Well, not about everything. Not about *me*!'

'Look——!'

He was so incensed that for a dangerous moment she imagined he was about to shake her by the shoulders. Instead he grabbed her arm in a painful grip and she felt the pressure of his fingers digging into her flesh. Wildly she struggled to free herself of his vice-like grip. 'Let me go! You're hurting me!'

His hand dropped away, but there was no mistaking the anger in his sun-bronzed face. Sarah drew a quick breath. Had she gone too far in defying his orders? Far enough to court instant dismissal at his hands? She rubbed her arm, still marked with the imprint of his fingers. 'All this about a bit of sunshine. It's ridiculous!'

'That's what you think?' His voice lashed her with suppressed fury.

'That's exactly what I think!' Never in all her life had she been so angry with anyone. 'Sunshine, and lots of it, is what I've been looking forward to in this country. Why should I shut it out?'

'Because I told you——'

'And I don't believe a word of those scare tactics of yours——'

'You don't?' He ground out the words. 'Go ahead, then!'

Two danger flags flared in her cheeks. 'I intend to.' She tossed her head defiantly, sending the dark hair flying around her cheeks. Then she stooped to snatch up a blue plastic bin lying at her feet and, without a backward glance, hurried towards the nearest row of vines.

For the first two hours she found the work enjoyable. She watched the way in which the other pickers selected and handled the grapes as they moved slowly down the leafy aisles. If she didn't much care for the spiders who had made their nests among the vines or wasps flying overhead at least she managed to conceal her dislike.

'Wow! It's going to be a scorcher today!' a girl picker a few feet ahead threw over her shoulder. 'Take a look at that!'

Sarah followed her gaze to the thermometer placed at the centre point of the row of vines.

'You're new here, aren't you?' The New Zealand girl smiled cheerfully.

'Mmm.' Sarah paused to put grapes in the container. 'From England, would you believe?'

The stranger laughed. 'Oh, I believe it, looking at you. You know something...?' She hesitated. 'You won't mind if I tell you?'

'Of course not.'

'You're going to be badly burned by the time the day's over.' She then said in some surprise, 'Didn't Nick fill you in about the right gear to wear for picking?'

Sarah lifted her small chin a fraction. It was a habit she seemed to have fallen into since arriving here. 'Yes, he did! And I told him I didn't have to do as he told me!' She couldn't help the note of defiance that tinged her voice.

The other girl laughed. 'Like that, is it? Look, I've got a cover-up blouse, long sleeves and all, and I've brought along a spare sun-visor too. You're welcome to use them if——'

'No, thanks.' Sarah shook her head. 'I'll be all right. I just can't wait to get a tan like the rest of you.'

The girl's round, cheerful face sobered. 'It'll be awfully painful——'

'I don't mind,' Sarah declared airily. 'It'll be worth it.' To change the subject she ran on, 'Tell me, what are those tiny birds fluttering among the vines?'

The girl gave up any further argument concerning the effects of the summer sun out here in the Pacific with its hole-in-the-ozone-layer atmosphere. 'Oh, they're fantails. Pretty, aren't they?'

But Sarah was no longer listening. 'Help!' Her scream rang through the air as she leaped backwards, overturning her bin and scattering grapes over the ground. Eyes dilated, she stared in fear and amazement at the great black insect with its long threatening feelers and high-jointed legs.

The girl she had been chatting with hurried to her side. 'Look!' Sarah was still shuddering. She shrieked again as the menacing feelers moved towards her. 'That evil, horrible——'

'What's the trouble? Someone pushed the panic button?' Nick came hurrying along the lane between the vines towards her. 'It's you, Sarah!' He came to stand at her side. 'Did a wasp get you?'

'Not a wasp——' She was still trembling with fright. 'It's an awful *thing*! It crawled out of the vines and attacked me!' She rubbed her wrist where a crimson spot marked the white translucent skin.

'You probably disturbed his nest,' Nick said. 'Let me see the damage.'

Sarah flung out her arm and he looked down at her with a grin. 'Nothing serious.' Heartless brute! 'The old weta looks a lot more fearsome than he is. It's the long feelers that make him look so ferocious. He'll give you a nip if he's cornered, but he's a lot more scared of you than you are of him.'

'You reckon?' She could have kicked herself in humiliation. Putting on such a performance, making all that fuss about a harmless insect—well, practically harmless, even if it did look absolutely horrifying. And wouldn't you know, she thought crossly, that the boss would be right on the spot to witness her display of needless terror!

'Take a break in the shade of the trees,' he was saying, 'and I'll get the first-aid kit from the house, just to be on the safe side.' He led the way between the vines, and for once Sarah offered no objection to his high-handed way of ordering her around.

Out in the air with its fresh tang of the pines she found it a relief to drop down on the grass. It seemed no time at all before Nick was back with her, a tube of medicated cream in his hand.

As he bent over her, smoothing the antiseptic cream over the red mark on her wrist, his dark hair brushed her cheek and his touch set up a trembling in her over which she seemed to have no control. Pray heaven he would put it down to the effects of her recent experience among the vines! At that moment he raised his head. For a second tiny flames flickered in his eyes and she knew that he was well aware of the effect his touch was having on her, damn him! Wildly she rushed into speech. 'That made me feel quite shaky. I guess I'm not used to insects that size.' Or to a man who can set my senses alight by the merest touch of his fingers. The thought came unbidden.

She wrenched her mind back to the deep, drawling tones.

'You'll get used to them,' he murmured offhandedly. 'Feel like getting back to the job? If you'd rather——'

'Of course I do!' she asserted, and threw in for good measure, 'I've wasted enough time as it is!'

As they moved away together to join the pickers moving slowly between the rows of greenery she wondered if she had merely imagined that fleeting expression in his dark eyes.

As the sun rose higher in the cloudless blue dome of the sky the stifling humidity of the atmosphere in the closed-in lanes between the vines increased. Sarah, as she wiped away the perspiration that was trickling down her neck, was aware of a burning sensation on her unprotected skin of face, arms and throat.

The fruit drinks that Kate brought down to the pickers at intervals throughout the morning were icy and delicious, and at the lunchtime break Sarah dropped down beside the other women in the shade of a giant macrocarpa tree. The pickers shared their sandwiches with her and she sipped the chilled fruit drinks thankfully.

Her companions were a cheerful, friendly group of women. Eagerly they plied Sarah with questions about life in England. Had she attended the London exhibitions and theatre shows of which they had read in travel magazines?

Sarah shook her head. 'I don't live in London, and it costs an awful lot to travel there and stay overnight to see a show.'

'Yes, I suppose it does.' It was an aspect of living in England that hadn't previously occurred to them. 'I expect you had to save like mad,' someone said, 'to be able to afford to come halfway across the world for a working holiday out here?'

Nervously she looked away, plucking at the grass at her feet. She felt a little sick at the thought that she was deceiving these kindly folk who had shown her how to pick the grapes from the vines and were so concerned with the effects of the hot sun on her fair English skin.

A laughing feminine voice broke in on her unhappy musing. 'Lucky for you, Sarah, that Kate didn't take you for the girl who's inherited Sunvalley!' Sarah froze, the food she was swallowing turning to a hard lump in her throat. 'They say she lives in England,' the girl ran on chattily, 'but if she does the lawyers over there don't seem to be able to find her. It must be over a year now since Steven died. Maybe they never will locate her——'

'And Nick will be able to stay at Sunvalley for good and things will go on just the same as ever,' another voice broke in cheerfully.

'It wouldn't be the same,' another woman pointed out. 'Oh, sure he's manager here, but he's not the owner. He should be by rights, but he's not. He's just filling in until *she* turns up.'

A wistful feminine voice said softly, 'Maybe she'll come out here and Nick will fall madly in love with her and they'll get married and he'll be a real partner again, just as he was with Steven.'

'Don't be stupid!' came a chorus of derisive voices. 'Can you really see Nick pocketing his pride and getting the vineyard back on those terms? It would put him in the position of a fortune-hunter—well, that's the way he'd see it.'

'But he's rapt in Sunvalley. He might——'

'Never!'

'But if he loved her, really loved her, I mean——'

'It wouldn't make any difference, not to Nick. Imagine him asking the girl who owned the place to marry him! That's the last thing he'd do even if he were in love with her. You know his pride!'

'Anyway,' a calm new voice said, 'he could be still in love with Lynn.' Now Sarah was unashamedly listening, she couldn't seem to help herself. 'Every now and again you see them together, and neither of them has married anyone else. You know those kind of romances when a couple don't seem to be happy together yet miss each other when they're apart!'

The voices blurred in Sarah's ears. She was feeling very strange, almost ill, although she would never admit it to anyone. A blinding headache throbbed at her temples and a wasp sting she had thought would not worry her over-much was now throbbing more painfully than at the time of the attack.

A friendly voice broke in on her thoughts. 'Is that wasp sting you collected a while back worrying you?' enquired a round-faced, red-haired girl. 'I'll put something on it.' Drawing a small phial from the pocket of her well-worn jeans, she proceeded to dab liquid on the red spot on Sarah's ankle. 'You're all right, aren't you?' Suddenly her kindly tones held a note of urgency, for Sarah's face had paled beneath the hot colour in her cheeks.

With an effort she pulled herself together and the moment of dizziness passed. 'I'm fine—honestly!'

Afterwards Sarah could recall little of the endless afternoon beyond a blurred impression of heat and pain and discomfort. At last, the interminable day's picking was over, the final bucket of grapes picked up by Nick in the tractor and taken to the cellar. Blindly Sarah stumbled up the path to the cottage and threw herself down on the bed.

Soiled and dishevelled, stained with purple grape juice and damp with perspiration, she was aware of nothing but a sickening headache, pain in her back and a sense of her skin being on fire. With the dusk came a cooling of the atmosphere, yet strangely she was feeling hotter than ever. And thirsty—so thirsty.

At some time during the hours of darkness she had a hazy impression of a glass being held to her lips and an authoritative voice saying, 'Drink it, it'll bring down the fever.' She had a sensation of a blessedly ice-cold cloth being held to her throbbing forehead, of cool sheets, the touch of soothing ointment on her burning skin, and then she slipped back to merciful oblivion.

CHAPTER FOUR

PINK streamers of dawn trailed across the eastern sky when Sarah came back to consciousness. For a time she lay motionless, trying to fit the pieces of the puzzle together as hazy impressions of the past few hours drifted through her mind.

One thing she knew for sure, and that was that she was feeling much better. A little groggy maybe, she admitted to herself as she dropped to the floor. A drink of water was what she craved. She moved into the adjoining room that was the kitchen, then stood still. Could she be still suffering from the illusions of the night? she wondered, staring at Nick. Clad in yesterday's work-stained clothes, he was lying on the couch, his dark hair rumpled and his head turned aside.

Noiselessly she moved on bare feet to the sink, filled a glass from the cold-water tap, then turned to find him watching her, his gaze dark and intent.

'Sarah! You're all right!' He sprang to his feet, his eyes luminous with an emotion she couldn't define. Relief? Impossible, she told herself the next moment.

'Yes, of course I am!' She shook back her hair, heavy with perspiration and dust. 'What are you doing here?' she asked stupidly. The next moment enlightenment came. 'I get it,' she said slowly. 'You've been here all night?'

'That's right,' came the drawling tones. 'Thought you might need someone around. You happened to be delirious——'

She raised heavy-lidded eyes in amazement. 'Delirious?'

The next moment warning bells rang in her mind. Suppose her unguarded tongue had given away the secret she must not reveal and she had ruined everything? She said on a sharp indrawn breath, 'What did I say? I mean . . . I suppose I—talked a lot of nonsense?'

'You sure did. Yelling blue murder was more like it! You were screaming for help, calling out something about wetas chasing you around the room. You sounded as if you were taking part in a horror movie! I thought I'd better stick around just to make sure you were OK.'

She let out her breath on a sigh of relief. Everything was all right, then; her secret was still safe. Dropping down to a chair, she sipped the cold water. 'I don't know what happened to me last night.'

'You collected a spot of sunstroke, that's all.' She waited for him to say, 'I told you so,' but he didn't. 'You had a raging fever for a while, but that's all over now, by the look of things.'

'Golly!' Sarah caught sight of her reflection in the mirror on the bureau—tangled hair, eyes with dark smudges around them and face and arms and shoulders all an unattractive shade of deep crimson. 'I look awful!' she gasped, then swung around to face him. 'But I'm going to help with the harvesting today! I'll take a cool shower and I'll be as good as new.' All at once it seemed terribly important that she should not let him down. Because she had already let him down so badly, even though he was unaware of her deception. 'I've got to get back to work,' she insisted frantically. 'I promised.'

Nick regarded her speculatively. 'No picking,' he told her, and she knew he meant what he said. 'Forget it,' he went on as she made to rush into speech, 'I've got someone else lined up for the job.'

'What *can* I do, then?' Her tone was sharp with urgency.

'No need for you to do anything.' His voice was strangely gentle. 'Tomorrow will be soon enough to think about work.'

'No!' she persisted. 'I want to get back to work today.'

He shrugged broad shoulders. 'You can put in an hour or so in the office later if you feel up to it. See how you feel.' All at once he was very much her employer, cool, impersonal, matter-of-fact. Could he really be the same man who had seen her through the nightmare hours of the night?

'Thanks,' she said awkwardly.

His lazy, amused grin was one he seemed to keep just for her. 'For what?'

For a moment she hesitated. 'You know,' she said very low, 'getting me over the sunstroke.'

'Oh, that.' A quizzical smile played around his lips. 'I just kept the dragons away.'

Sarah's green eyes twinkled and she threw him a teasing smile. 'A knight in shining armour?' And could have bitten her tongue out the next moment as she found herself at the receiving end of his cool stare.

'Something like that. Kate did her bit to help out.' His flat tones had the effect of making her feel like a child rebuffed by an adult. Now she was glad of the sunburn that masked the hot colour she could feel flooding her cheeks.

For heaven's sake, she raged inwardly, did he have some mistaken idea that she was making up to him? No doubt it was a reaction he had come to expect from romantic young women brought within the influence of his masculine charisma and dark good looks. But this girl? Never! It was going to be difficult enough to play her part while working alongside him during the following weeks without the additional hazard of any emotional entanglement to complicate matters. It wasn't as if he held any real attraction for her. Well, honesty compelled her to admit, nothing she couldn't handle.

She became aware of his deep tones. 'Take things easy for today. You can take over the office work from now on and help out with customers in the bottle store, right? See you there tomorrow.'

'No!' she flung at him. 'I'll be there today!'

'If you're sure you feel up to it,' he said reluctantly, and she could almost hear the unspoken words: You never learn, do you, Sarah?

Aloud she said brightly and confidently, 'Of course I feel up to it! I'm quite all right now.'

'You sure are a devil for punishment,' he told her with a sceptical grin, and turned away.

Alone in the room Sarah told herself that she just *had* to feel well again. The strange, unfamiliar sensation of light-headedness would soon pass, and all that really mattered was that she prove a point to her overbearing employer.

A cool shower dealt with grape-juice stains, dust and perspiration, and was infinitely refreshing, and soft rainwater showered in a jet on her lathered hair left her dark locks soft and silky. After towelling herself dry on one of Kate's fluffy towels she managed a reasonably successful repair job with her painfully reddened skin. A lotion she found on the bedside table proved to be cool and soothing on her inflamed cheeks, and it was amazing what make-up could do in the way of concealing sun-damage. It would be worth it all, she consoled herself, once she had attained the deep tan on her skin that New Zealand girls and men seemed to take for granted.

Presently she was pulling on bra and panties, fastening denim jeans around her slim waist, and pulling over her head a shirt of thin white cotton, the long sleeves and high coolie neckline protecting her painfully reddened arms and shoulders. Then she mixed a mug of instant coffee, toasted a slice of wholemeal bread and spread it with kiwi-fruit jam she found in the refrigerator.

Outside in the crystal-clear morning air she made her way along the bush-shaded pathway towards the room Nick called his office. There was no one in sight, and she seated herself at the typewriter and proceeded to make herself conversant with the machine. It took her only a short time to feel confident about her typing and she turned her attention to the invoices scattered over the desk. She had just completed the task of sorting them into alphabetical order when a shadow fell over the open doorway and the next moment Nick came striding towards her.

'Sarah!' he exclaimed.

'Don't look so surprised!' She made her smile extra bright. 'I told you I'd be here.'

His gaze moved to the neatly piled invoices. 'And bang on time!' She felt inordinately pleased at the note of surprise and satisfaction in his tone. 'Right! For starters this lot can go in the post.' He was bending towards her, so close that she caught the faint tang of male cologne. 'Better check first to make sure the accounts haven't been settled in the last week or so.'

'I'll do that.' She glanced up to meet the full impact of his dark eyes, alight with an expression she couldn't define. All at once she was acutely *aware* of him. If only he didn't sense the confusion of her senses or the strange excitement that was quivering through her.

The next moment she told herself that she need not have concerned herself, for his drawling tones were quite unperturbed, his voice that of an employer detailing office duties to a new employee.

'Come over to the bottle store,' he was saying, 'and I'll fill you in about the sales work.'

In the small room where the walls were lined with shelves stocked with wine bottles he led her to the long counter. 'There's not much to it, prices don't vary except for the Kiwi-fruit Cooler. I get the fruit from the kiwi-fruit plantation next door, take it off their hands when it happens to be the wrong shape or size for the overseas export markets. No need for you to sort through different varieties,' he explained. 'Except for the odd bottle of Kiwi-fruit Cooler there's only one line they'll be interested in here, and that's the Sunvalley Red.'

'I know.' Her green eyes mocked him. 'To achieve perfection the wine-maker needs to concentrate on only one variety. You told me.'

He threw her an enigmatic glance. 'You're learning.'

She couldn't tell whether or not he was being sarcastic, but to be on the safe side she decided to teach him a lesson. Schooling her voice to a light note, she said brightly, 'I could tell you something else that would improve things—in the sales line, I mean.' Ignoring the expression of sceptical amusement in his eyes, she waved a hand towards the small high windows. 'All those cobwebs! Those windows need a good wash, and the floor could do with a scrub and a polish too.' She added with feeling, 'I know if it were mine——' She stopped abruptly, horrified at what she was saying, but to her relief Nick didn't appear to notice the sudden break in her voice.

He merely murmured offhandedly, 'Oh, Kate sees to all that.'

Her eyes were shooting sparks. 'Are you sure?'

His lips tightened ominously. Now he was angry with her all over again, and it was all her own fault. Remember, she chided herself, you're lucky to have found a job of any sort here. Trouble with you, girl, is that you've got into the habit of thinking of the vineyard as your property and you're in charge here right now. Forget it!

'Morning!' called a feminine voice, and Kate came into the room, her shrewd gaze darting to Sarah's flushed cheeks. 'How are you feeling now, Sarah? I didn't expect to see you in the office today.'

'I'm all right now, thanks.' Who would have thought, Sarah marvelled, that the fiery-tempered little woman of their first meeting could be so genuinely sympathetic? Look at the way in which she had tended her last night. Aloud she said, 'I should be, with the good care I had through the night. That medicated cream you put on me really took the sting out of the burning. It eased the pain so much.'

'Me?' Kate's mouth opened in surprise. 'It wasn't——' Sarah threw Nick a startled look, then, meeting his mocking glance, wished she hadn't glanced his way. She wrenched her mind back to Kate's rapid tones. 'Don't thank me. I had a migraine last night, and it was Nick who came to your rescue and stayed up all night, giving you aspirin every few hours to bring your temperature down. All I did was supply the medication and hand out fresh sheets from the linen cupboard every now and again.'

Oh, no! Sarah was sick with mortification and the realisation that it had been Nick who had smoothed the healing cream over her burning body. If only it had been Kate who had attended to her needs. With seething anger she reflected that one way or another Nick always seemed to gain an advantage over her. And that, she vowed silently, was something she intended to change—and soon!

Green fire sparkled in her eyes as she glanced towards him, and, just as she had expected, he was enjoying her discomfiture, the devil! A tide of anger flooded through her and she caught her lower lip with her teeth, determined not to allow him the satisfaction of knowing how furious she was with him.

Becoming aware of Kate's interested glance, all she could do was to glare at him silently. The expression of amusement in his lively dark eyes did nothing in the way of defusing her anger.

Apparently, however, Kate noticed nothing amiss. She was chatting happily to Sarah. 'Aren't we lucky with the weather? A few more days will mean the end of the harvesting, and it looks as if the sunshine will go on for a while yet.'

'By the way,' Nick said, 'I've put Sarah in charge of the office and looking after customers in the wine store.' He turned to Sarah. 'The urgent job will be for you to get invitations out and ring the city newspapers about the wine-festival day at the end of the week. You'll need to contact the caterers we had for last year's wing-ding and ring through invitations to anyone you can contact by phone, otherwise post out invitations. I've already organised entertainment—Darren will take care of that. I booked him up last year for the festival day. I'll give him a buzz to confirm this year's date, make sure he turns up and brings his guitar with him. He's a hard guy to contact.'

'He worked in the vineyard for a while,' Kate told Sarah.

'When it suited him,' Nick said drily. 'You'll find the festival-day invitation list in the desk drawer in the office, Sarah. I'll go over it with you later.'

When he had left the room Kate said thoughtfully, 'You can't help liking Darren. He's got a way with him and his singing voice seems to tear you apart. Trouble is, he's just not reliable. He would work for a while, then he'd be off somewhere else. You could never depend on him. Not like Nick,' her voice softened. 'When it comes to anything to do with Sunvalley he's really...' She paused, searching for a word.

'Dedicated?' suggested Sarah, adding, tight-lipped, 'I've noticed.'

'You'll enjoy the festival day,' Kate told her. 'Folks come from all parts of the country each year. It's fun.'

A short while later, when Sarah rang through to the first name on the invitation list, a cheerful male voice answered her call.

'Hello? Larry Matthews here.'

'Hello! I'm ringing from Sunvalley Vineyard,' Sarah said in her clear young tones, 'to let you know our annual wine festival is being held on the eighteenth of this month. Nick asked me to tell you he's looking forward to meeting you at the festival. You'll be there?'

'Will *you*?' The boyish tones were threaded with interest.

'Of course. I work here.'

An infectious chuckle echoed over the wire. 'And you're fresh out from England? I can tell by your voice. Fear not, I'll be there, if only for the pleasure of meeting you—what did you say your name was?'

'I didn't. I'm Sarah——'

'Nice name—I like it. If you're half as nice as you sound——'

'Bye, Larry.' Sarah was still smiling as she replaced the receiver in its cradle.

Later in the day she was working her way through the list of names when she looked up to meet the smiling glance of a short, fair-haired girl, obviously pregnant, who was standing in the doorway.

'Hi!' The girl came into the room. 'I guess you're Sarah, the English girl?'

'That's me,' Sarah said in her open, friendly way. 'I've just landed a job here.'

'I know—I've heard all about it. I'm Penny, by the way, and Bill's my husband. We live next door—the kiwi-fruit orchard, you know? My goodness!' She took in Sarah's reddened face. 'You did get a dose of sunburn yesterday! Were you out in the vines, picking?'

Sarah nodded.

'And Nick didn't warn you about the dangerously hot sun out in this part of the world?' Penny said incredulously.

'Well, actually——' Sarah was heartily sick of the conversation which had taken on an all too familiar theme. She avoided the other girl's enquiring gaze.

But Penny only laughed. 'A bit overbearing, was he? Handing out oodles of unasked-for advice? I can imagine. He can be like that sometimes, but he's still a great guy. You couldn't have a better boss to work under. Staying long?' And, before Sarah could make a reply, 'A working holiday, is that the story?'

'I'm staying for the summer.' Mentally Sarah added, If I'm lucky! 'I want to get some experience in a vineyard,' her voice rang with enthusiasm, 'find out all I can about the growing of the grapes, the bottling, everything.'

'You do sound keen. Not thinking of taking it up as a career, are you?'

'No, no.' Sarah told herself sternly that she would have to watch her tongue in future.

But she had no need to worry, for Penny had forgotten the subject the next minute. She was pushing the long fair hair back from behind her ears. 'Oh, I almost forgot what I came for—a bottle of Nick's famous red. We're having friends in to dinner tonight and they prefer it to any other. Did you know Nick won the accolade for the country's most prestigious red? Not bad for a small vineyard like this, is it?'

Sarah didn't answer. She was becoming awfully weary of hearing of Nick's efficiency, Nick's dedication to his work, Nick's red wine. Instead she murmured, 'I'll get it for you,' and moved into the bottle store.

Penny paid for the wine and was on the point of leaving when she paused to throw over her shoulder, 'I suppose you've heard the story about Sunvalley?' Without waiting for an answer she swept on, 'By rights Nick should own the vineyard instead of being just the manager, and on a temporary basis at that! He would have been if Steven hadn't put off altering his will. He always spoke of Nick inheriting the estate, but he didn't ever get around to updating the will. Would you believe, everything goes to some girl over in England whom he only met a few times umpteen years ago?'

Sarah could find no words, but fortunately Penny didn't appear to notice her silence. 'The awful part of it all is that Nick is rapt in the place. To him it isn't just his home, it's the centre of his life. He thinks of nothing but the vineyard, especially since he and Lynn——'

'Lynn?' queried Sarah.

'The girl he was engaged to. The engagement was broken off the day we got the news about Nick not inheriting the vineyard. Personally I thought he had a lucky escape,' added Penny. 'Lynn won the Miss New Zealand Beauty Queen title that year and she's quite lovely to look at, of course—that is if you go for that cold, fair, statuesque type. I guess Nick still loves her. It's over a year ago now since the break-up and he never seems interested in any other girl. Heavens——' she glanced down at her wristwatch '—is that the time? Bill will be in for his morning cuppa. I'll have to fly! See you!'

Sarah stared after her unseeingly, her thoughts racing in confusion. She was assailed by a sick feeling of guilt and a queer sense of regret. Should she confess the truth to Nick, relinquish all claim to the property? It was what she ought to do, she knew, and yet...

Wait, a small voice piped in her mind, don't do anything in a rush. Stay on for the summer, act as if nothing had happened to change your feelings about the legacy. As if you're just any girl from England out here on a working holiday.

As the long day went on Sarah stuck determinedly to her office tasks, telling herself that the heat of which she was unpleasantly aware would be a hundred times more intense down in the humidity of the rows of vines where the team of workers was picking. Once or twice during the afternoon a feeling of faintness threatened to overwhelm her, but she battled on, cursing herself for her fumbling fingers and the typing errors she was making more and more frequently.

'Time for you to call it a day,' called a richly masculine voice, and she glanced up to see Nick approaching her with his long, leisurely stride. She welcomed the suggestion. After all, it wouldn't do any harm to give in to his peremptory orders, not just this once.

'Thought you might like some refreshment.' He was pouring fresh mango juice into a glass. He handed it to her, and she enjoyed the delicious sensation of the ice-cold juice sliding down her throat.

Pouring a glass of juice for himself, he dropped down to a stool. 'How are the invitations coming along?' he asked.

'I've got them all ready to post.' It was amazing how different she was feeling, almost as if his air of vigour and well-being had rubbed off on her, giving her fresh energy.

'Great.' Nick set down his glass. 'I put a phone call through to Darren and had a word with him. Seems he's had an argument with a truck on the motorway and crashed his car again. He tells me he's not too badly hurt, but he's just left hospital and may not be able to make it to the festival this year. I've buzzed a few other possibilities, but no luck, so...' He sent her the heart-stopping grin that in spite of his maddening ways had the effect of sending her into an emotional spin, a state of mind, new to Sarah, where anything could happen. She made an effort to concentrate on his rich masculine tones. 'That's where you might have to come into the picture.'

'Me?' She was trying to gather her wits together. 'You mean you need me at the festival to entertain guests?'

'Could do.' His dark eyes were glowing. 'If Darren doesn't show up, how about filling in for him in the entertainment department? All you need to do is to sing a few numbers—one happens to be rather special: a sort of folk-song.' Carelessly he added, 'Nothing you won't be able to handle.'

'I told you I'd sing and play the guitar for guests,' she said carefully. 'Is that all you want from me?'

'From you, Sarah?' For a fractional moment a lambent flame leaped in his eyes, to be instantly extinguished. 'Just a song,' he drawled, 'for the moment.' Before she could make any comment he was running on, 'I've brought along the music, so you can get a line on it beforehand, make yourself familiar with the tune. You'll really go for it once you've tried it out.'

Reluctantly Sarah took the faded sheet of music he was holding towards her and scanned it. She said in surprise, 'The words are in another language.'

'Not to worry.' He shrugged away the problem. 'The English translation is pencilled in below the other.'

She eyed him warily. 'Is it a Yugoslav song?'

'Sort of. All about the tough times the first European settlers had to put up with when they came to live in this country. Should be right in your line.' He raised deceptively innocent dark brows. 'You did tell me you sang folk-songs, ballads, all that stuff?'

'Yes, I do, but——'

He went on unheedingly, 'Steven had it sung every year at the end-of-the-season festival day in the vineyard. I guess it's got to be a tradition around here.' All at once his voice deepened. 'Especially this year.'

Because it would be his last festival day here in Sunvalley? The words hung silently between them, but she dared not pursue that line of thought.

'Right! That's all taken care of.' Sarah could feel prickles of resentment rising in her at his high-handed manner. His do-as-I-say tones were more in the nature of a downright order than a request.

'No!' Her green eyes sparkled defiantly. Why should she agree to sing his strange, unfamiliar song just because he told her—correction, ordered her to? 'You'll have to get someone else to sing it!' she flung at him.

His mouth tightened with anger and a muscle jerked at the side of his cheek. 'Part of the deal,' he reminded her inexorably, 'or have you forgotten?'

'Oh, I know I promised to sing and play the guitar for you,' she exploded breathlessly, 'but only if the songs were ones familiar to me or melodies I'd composed myself.' She shot him a triumphant glance. 'Do *you* remember?' The darkening of his expression left her in no doubt on that score.

'When it comes to singing words in some foreign language, even if it's translated, and playing a song I've never even heard of——' Having given full rein to her feelings, she couldn't seem able to stop. 'Just because you...' her voice lurched and she hurried on '...want me to! Well, I'm not going along with it. I'll do the entertaining because I said I would, but I'll only sing songs I know.'

'Is that right?' Anger throbbed in his low tones. 'If you weren't still on the sick list——'

'What would you do?' she taunted. 'Shake some sense into me? Throw me out of the house?' Heavens, she thought in dismay, what if he does just that? And she held her breath.

Instead he said with deadly softness, 'Keep the music.' Deftly he slipped the sheet of music into the pocket of her jeans. 'You'll change your mind about it when you're feeling better.'

'I won't, you know!' Why was she trembling?

She braced herself for his cutting rejoinder, but without another word he turned and left her, and suddenly the room seemed deadly quiet and strangely empty. She brushed aside the absurd thought. She had had enough, more than enough, of her dominating, arrogant, utterly insufferable employer! Without pausing even to tidy the papers scattered over the desk she hurried from the room, slamming the door behind her.

CHAPTER FIVE

IN THE morning Sarah was back in the office on time, a pile of newsletters lying on the desk before her. Even as her gaze slid down the mailing list, however, her thoughts drifted. She told herself that all she needed to do in order to avoid the pitfalls of her life here was to regard the period as a normal working holiday in another country.

So far the plan had worked—well, most of the time. If only it weren't for Nick. The disturbing effect the man had on her was quite absurd. She could only blame the powerful aura of masculine attraction he projected. Why, merely finding herself in the same room with him made her feel piercingly, crazily aware of him. A mere physical thing, of course. It was just that never before had she found herself in a situation that she couldn't seem able to cope with. Her only defence was to avoid him as much as possible—if she could. It was difficult, though, like right at this moment.

Through the open doorway she watched him approach from the vineyard in the valley, his lean, well-muscled figure taking the grassy slope in swift strides. As he came nearer she could see that he looked alert and happy, whistling a tune as he neared the office. Mentally she braced herself. If he was congratulating himself on her having changed her mind about singing his precious folk-song at the festival she would very soon disillusion him on that score!

'Morning, Sarah!' He paused in the doorway, the morning sunlight forming a nimbus around his soft dark hair. 'How are you feeling?'

She pulled a face. 'Peeling.'

He advanced into the room, his assessing gaze sweeping her reddened arms and throat to move upwards and linger on her face. 'That stage won't last for long. Soon you'd never believe you'd copped that outsized dose of sunburn in one go.'

'No, you wouldn't,' she agreed ruefully, 'and I haven't even got a Kiwi tan to show for it!'

'You can forget about a tan,' he told her, and she stiffened at his peremptory tones, 'with that peaches-and-cream skin of yours.' She moved restlessly beneath his searching gaze. If only he'd stop looking at her.

Dropping down to the desk, he perched on a corner, swinging a sun-bronzed leg. 'I've got a job lined up for you, a spot of weekend work,' he told her.

'That's all right. If it's figure work I don't mind catching up with the books. It's been a bit slow, working on the tax—it's all new to me, but I'm getting used to it. And weekends are no different to me from any other day.'

He grinned. 'This one will be. I've just had a phone call from Darren, the guy who provides the music for the wind-up after harvesting. He was all apologies for not being able to make it for the wingding, but I told him to concentrate on getting better, that I had someone else booked up for the day. No problem.'

'You did?' Sarah tilted her small chin. The curt manner in which he had demanded she sing an unknown song, his hot anger when she had refused, still rankled. 'I'm not so sure now that I want to do it——'

His hard stare was unnerving. 'We had all that out when you applied for work here,' he reminded her coolly. 'You seemed rapt in the idea then. I did warn you about this possibility coming up——'

'I'd like to have more time to practise my songs,' she said tightly, 'if I'm to play in public.'

He waved aside her objection with the lift of a well-shaped hand. 'Why? The audience won't be a critical lot. A free show, with wine and food laid on. I don't know what you're worrying about.'

'No, you wouldn't!' she flung at him, tight-lipped. 'Anyway,' she swept on with heightened colour beneath the sunburn, 'how about a guitar? I haven't brought mine with me.'

'It's all taken care of.' His mocking grin was maddening to her taut nerves. 'One of Kate's nieces keeps a spare guitar here. She likes to have it when she comes to stay in the holidays.' Carelessly, he added, 'It's kicking around the house some place. I'll look it up for you.'

Sarah shot him an exasperated glance. If he expected her to give a public performance on any old guitar that happened to be lying around the place... Oh, he was insufferable!

'Don't look like that!' The rich masculine tones broke across her rebellious thoughts. 'It's a good instrument and it was tuned just the other day. You'll like it.'

She sent him a scorching glance. Of all the self-opinionated males she had ever come across! Aloud she forced her voice to a casual note. 'I'll see if I can play it, otherwise——' she shrugged slim shoulders '—it's just no go!'

The threat had no effect on him whatever. He simply murmured offhandedly, 'Oh, you'll be OK.' Callous devil!

Suddenly he dropped to the floor. 'Look, I've got to go, but I'll be back in a minute.'

Sarah glared at him silently, but the angry light in her green eyes spelled out the message plainly: As if I care!

In a short time he was moving back along the path to the office, and once again she caught the rhythm of that unfamiliar tune he was whistling. She pretended to busy herself with the mailing list, not glancing up until he had come to stand at her side.

'Brought you something!' She looked up to meet the devilish gleam in his dark eyes that she didn't trust one little bit. 'I thought you could do with it.'

All at once Sarah felt her tense nerves relax. A peace-offering, she thought, a way of letting her know that he was sorry for the cursory treatment he had handed out to her this morning.

'Thank you!' she said warmly, and fell right into the trap. 'What is it?' As always her gaze fell, unable to sustain the brilliance of his look.

'This.' Bending to the floor, he picked up a guitar and laid it on the desk in front of her. 'It's yours to use while you're here.'

She hesitated, eyeing him warily. 'And I play any melody I choose? Songs I'm familiar with?'

'But of course,' came his drawling tones. 'What else?'

Picking up the instrument, she fingered the strings. 'This is a terribly expensive guitar—one from South Mexico. I've never played on anything like this.'

Nick didn't seem surprised. 'Only the best for Elaine. She teaches music at a college in the city.'

'And she won't mind my using it?'

'Why should she? As I said, it's yours while you're here.'

Sarah bent over the guitar, plucking the strings. 'You're taking a risk, aren't you, with me? How do you know I won't let you down at the festival? Ruin your big day?'

'Not to worry. The crowd won't be in a mood to be critical of the entertainment, especially by the end of the day.'

'Really?' She twanged a note viciously. 'It's hardly worth the bother of my playing for them, then!' she flung at him, and set down the instrument.

'Part of the deal,' he reminded her blandly. 'I seem to recall your telling me——'

'All right! *All right*!' Oh, he made her so annoyed! With an effort she forced back the angry words that trembled on her lips. She said tightly, 'I won't have much time to practise anything special.'

'Just play something you know. I'll leave it to you.'

Sarah's soft lips tightened. His casual attitude regarding her skills as an entertainer was infuriating. But she would prove to him that she was worth every cent of his beastly pay. If only she hadn't opened her mouth regarding her entertainment experience—a modest enough record when you came right down to it: performances at a few private parties, a summer concert a year ago, the wind-up social gathering at the end of the year in the office where she had worked.

'Right! That about wraps it up!' he said.

The arrogance of him! she thought, fuming. 'If I decide to go along with it!' she said belatedly, and knew by the mocking glint in his eyes that she had betrayed herself, for she had to admit that she had agreed to entertain at his social function, damn him!

She wrenched her mind back to his vibrant tones. 'Tell me, what have you got in the way of gear? A long dress? Something with a spot of homespun glamour? You've played in public before—you'll know the sort of thing I mean.'

'Oh, I know exactly the type of dress you mean.' She took a wicked delight in being unable to do as he asked—ordered, rather—even when it came to a matter of her own clothes. 'But I didn't bring much with me—only working gear, jeans, T-shirts, shorts, that sort of stuff.'

'That's no use——' Nick waved away the garments as of no consequence. 'What I have in mind is something a bit different. It's OK, though. There's a traditional costume you can wear somewhere in the cottage—could be it's still hanging up in the wardrobe there. Darren's girlfriend brought it with her when she accompanied him on the guitar at last year's festival.' His frank appraisal of Sarah's slender form sent the tell-tale colour rushing to her cheeks. 'Should be just about your fit. You can try it on for size.'

'No, thanks!' She drew a ragged breath and strove to control her temper. Of all the nerve! What if he did happen to be her employer? That didn't give him the right to interfere in her private life.

All at once his expression softened. 'Believe me, you'll look a whole lot more attractive in that dress than Darren's partner!'

Compliments! And from Nick of all men! She could scarcely believe her ears. She eyed him suspiciously, but apparently his opinion in the matter was quite impersonal. She might have known.

The next moment surprise gave way to anger and two danger flags burned in her cheeks. 'Do you really think,' she exploded breathlessly, 'that I'd get myself all dressed up in some other girl's hand-me-down for this—this gathering of yours?'

'Vintage party, we call it,' he drawled.

Somehow she was finding it easier to throw down her challenge to his high-handed tactics when she didn't meet the full impact of his penetrating hard stare. 'Just to please you?' she added.

'Why not?' His voice was dangerously quiet.

His lips were tightly set and anger smouldered in his eyes. He was keeping his temper on a leash, she thought. You could tell by the way he ground out the words. Clearly the boss wasn't accustomed to having his commands treated lightly. Well, it was time he learned that the vineyard at the back of beyond that he set such store by might be his own little world, but it wasn't hers. At least, she amended silently, not yet.

'I take it . . .' his low, throbbing tones betrayed barely suppressed fury '. . . that you have no intention of changing your mind about this?'

'Never! Any more than I'd sing that old folk-song of yours, even if I did know it.'

'I can soon put you right with that.'

'Don't bother!' Sarah took a deep breath and summoned her fighting spirit. 'I'll play for you and sing a few songs if you want me to—English folk-songs, popular hit tunes everyone knows and can sing along with if they wish.' Her eyes were shooting sparks. 'But the last thing I'll be wearing at your festival will be a national costume.'

She was disconcertingly aware of the flush of hot colour staining her cheeks. Defiantly she threw up her chin—she seemed to be always doing that lately—only to catch the full force of his blazing stare. But she refused to allow herself to be intimidated by him. 'Anyway...' She tried to make her voice light and careless. 'I don't see why you should care so much. I mean, you're not really European—scarcely at all; you told me so yourself. You can scarcely owe allegiance to a country on the other side of the world. I don't see what all the fuss is about——'

'Don't you?' Anger throbbed in his low tones. 'Let me tell you.' In two strides he was beside her, his hands gripping her shoulders like steel bands. 'It's a tradition here. Do you understand?'

She struggled ineffectually in his grasp. 'I understand you're hurting me! Take your hands away from me!'

Nick freed her so suddenly that she all but lost her balance. She wrenched her mind back to his deep tones. 'I was hoping you might see reason——'

'Forget it!' She fought her way through the confusion of her senses. 'I'll tell you something! The day I wear that traditional costume of yours, and sing a song some New Zealander thought up all about gum-diggers in the early days, you'll know I've changed my mind! And that,' she flung at him triumphantly, 'is about as likely to happen as—as——' Wildly she searched her mind for the most unlikely possibility she could dream up, and at last came up with, 'My wanting to stay on here at Sunvalley forever—with you.'

With you? What was she saying? She could have kicked herself for the unfortunate turn of phrase, and she could tell by the satirical twist of Nick's lips that he hadn't missed the significance of her last two words.

He said with irony, 'Just so long as I know.'

She threw him a suspicious glance, but his bland stare gave nothing away. She could cheerfully have tossed the guitar at his dark, mocking face.

'Look.' In one of his swift changes of mood he bent towards her, and the brilliance of his gaze made her drop her eyes. 'I've got to take a run into town tomorrow—some marketing I've got to see to. Why don't I take you in with me? We'll drop in at a boutique in the city and pick up something in the way of a dress for you there.'

Really—she was still flushed and angry—he took too much for granted! The thought sparked her to say spiritedly, 'I'll come with you, but only if I can choose a dress for myself. I'll pay for it too, or I won't have one at all!' The possibility of finding herself in a situation where she might be in his debt didn't bear thinking about. 'I mean it!'

'All in the deal!' The mocking glint in his eyes made her feel more inflamed than ever. 'Pick you up at eight in the morning. Can you make it?'

'I guess so,' she said huffily. Only after he had left her did she fully realise just what she had let herself in for. A trip to Auckland and back would take the best part of a day. A day alone with Nick! By nature frank and outspoken, she would need to watch every word she spoke, knowing that one slip of the tongue could betray her true identity. No wonder that just being with him sent her into a state of nervous tension that she had never before experienced.

But never before had she met a man who sent her defences crumbling so that the only course left to her was to take evasive action and keep out of his way—if she could. In any event, it was too late now for regrets. She was committed.

The following day she was up early and waiting on the porch of the cottage when Nick braked the Land Rover to a stop on the track.

Watching him as he approached her over the grass, Sarah had to admit to herself that the boss was quite a man. You couldn't help but be aware of the aura of subdued power and sheer masculinity that he projected. Yet he appeared to be totally unaware of the effect he had on her—or on any other young and impressionable female who came in contact with his magnetic personality, she wouldn't wonder. Hastily she qualified the thought. Any girl, that was, who didn't have to work for him and who knew what he was really like. There was only one way to describe him, and that was downright bossy! And she should know!

'Morning!' he greeted her. 'You look right now as though you could take on the world!' His appreciative glance flickered over the dark-haired girl wearing a simple sleeveless dress of soft knitwear in a primrose shade, her eyes glimmering with a secret excitement.

She gave a guilty start and pushed aside the thoughts crowding her mind. 'It's the holiday feeling that accounts for it,' she told him.

'Holiday?' He slanted her a faintly quizzical grin.

'Working holiday, then,' she amended, smiling. She could even smile at Nick this morning. It must be something about the sparkling sunshiny day that was affecting her, she told herself.

He saw her seated in the Land Rover, then slammed the heavy door shut and moved around the vehicle to climb into the driver's seat. He put the Land Rover into gear and they swept along the track where thickly growing hibiscus bushes brushed the roof of the vehicle. At the foot of the slope they lurched over a rough bridge spanning a stream, then they were out on the highway where thickly growing native bush on either side threw long shadows over the road ahead.

It was amazing, she mused, that perched high in the seat of the Land Rover she was finding the trip so much more exciting and downright enjoyable than when seated in the luxurious coach in which she had travelled previously. But of course she had been travel-weary on that occasion, whereas now...

'You play things pretty close to the chest, don't you?' Nick's words startled her from her sense of dreamy content.

Once again warning bells rang in her mind. 'What do you mean?'

'Family and all that,' he murmured. 'You don't let on much about them.'

'Don't I?' Sarah moistened dry lips, playing for time. Could he be suspicious of her identity after all? She forced her voice to a careless note. 'That's because I haven't any—well, no one close. I live with my aunt,' she ran on, and held her breath as she awaited further questioning.

She realised the next minute, however, that her fears were groundless. Nick was merely showing a perfunctory interest in the matter. 'Most girls,' he was saying, 'prefer to make other living arrangements.' His gaze was fixed on the winding road ahead. A bird flew up from the sea of bush around them and soared to a tree-top. 'But you, you're quite happy living at home?'

'Yes, I am,' she asserted. 'I wouldn't stay if I weren't.' Why was he quizzing her like this about her home life?

His sideways glance went to her face. 'Or if you found someone you wanted to be with all the time?' he suggested in his maddening drawl.

'Well, I haven't,' she declared brightly, and realised the next moment that once again he had succeeded in extracting information from her regarding her personal life back home in England. Although why he should be so curious about her she couldn't imagine.

'Just checking.' The words were so low that afterwards she wondered if she had really heard them. Checking on what? A shaft of fear pierced her, but she forced the uneasy suspicions aside.

The sun had climbed high in the translucent blue bowl of the sky when Nick drew the vehicle to a shady spot off the road, a grassy area where far below a stream tumbled crystal-clear waters over rocks.

'Lunch break,' he announced briefly. Climbing out of the Land Rover, he waited to help her down from the high step on the passenger side of the vehicle. 'Jump and I'll catch you!' She caught his devastating grin. Could it be the lazy glint in the depths of his dark eyes that unnerved her, causing her to miss her footing and go plunging down into his waiting arms?

She was unprepared for the reaction his arms closing around her evoked, the raw force of his male attraction as she felt the soft curves of her body pressed against his sinewy chest that she could feel warm and hard through the cotton fabric of his shirt. He took his time about releasing her, and when he did she was breathing rapidly, her heartbeats uneven. She sneaked a glance at him from under her lashes, but apparently he was quite unaware of the effect his nearness had had on her, for he had turned away and was reaching into the Land Rover for a picnic hamper. That crazy moment when he had held her close hadn't meant a thing to him. She couldn't understand why she was feeling this sudden sense of let-down.

She dropped down on the dry grass and he came to kneel at her side. Opening a cool-box, he took out a bottle of fruit wine. In the hamper there were fluffy pikelets and pizza pie sealed in see-through cling-wrap, a carrot cake, luscious and tempting with its creamy lemon topping, kiwi-fruit and great yellow Golden Queen peaches from the orchard.

Sarah held out a plastic beaker and Nick poured wine into it. 'Tastes a lot better outside, wouldn't you say?'

She smiled. 'Oh, definitely! Do you know this is the first time I've ever tasted kiwi-fruit? Back where I come from they're awfully expensive in the shops.'

He grinned. 'Always a first time.' Slicing one of the pale green ovals in half, he handed her the fruit, and Sarah, as she scooped out the silvery green flesh, reflected that she couldn't remember when she had so much enjoyed a picnic lunch.

'I don't wonder *you* live at home,' she murmured teasingly, 'with a housekeeper who's a super cook like Kate——' She stopped short, realising by the darkening of his expression that she had said the wrong thing. Clearly her careless remark had evoked for him painful memories of a girl he had been about to marry a year ago, and whom he still loved. The thought came with a pang of the heart. He must still love her, that other girl, for surely a man of his calibre could attract the romantic interest of any girl he happened to fancy. Except this girl, of course—she was different!

'Let's get cracking, shall we?' said Nick shortly.

Out on the open highway once again Sarah forgot Nick's dark mood. As the miles fell away she was silent, wrapped in a deep sense of content laced somehow with excitement.

After a time bush-covered hills gave way to cleared farmlands dotted with grazing sheep. Soon she caught sight of deer enclosures with their soaring mesh fences and, later, the lush green slopes with their plantations of citrus and kiwi-fruit.

Soon they were moving through small scattered townships, then they swung into a motorway where the road cut across tidal waters with their thick mangrove swamps, moored pleasure boats and wading seabirds. Presently they turned off the winding motorway into a tree-lined city street, and Sarah, gazing towards the shimmering blue waters of the Auckland harbour, forgot her misgivings and annoyances, her irritation with the boss. All at once she was swept by a heightened sense of perception, joy and elation born of the novelty of her surroundings and the sheer magic of the sunshiny day.

Nick guided the Land Rover past a hillside park bright with flower gardens, then he edged the vehicle into a parking space in the street. He locked the vehicle and they strolled together along pavements thronged with shoppers. At the entrance to a mall with its attractively decorated stores Nick paused. 'I've got to look up a man in the office block over there——' He jerked his head towards a high-rise building with its mirror-glass blocks. 'You'll find a few boutiques right here,' he told her, 'and you might be lucky enough to pick up something you fancy.' He sent her the heart-knocking grin that she never seemed able to resist. 'Reckon you can find something you like in an hour?'

Sarah smiled up into his sun-darkened face. Today she was finding it very easy to forget how she really felt about him. She said laughingly, 'That depends on the price ticket.'

'Don't worry about it.' For a moment something flickered in his lively glance, then was gone. 'See you in an hour!'

Sarah opened her lips to protest. If he meant what she suspected he did—but it was too late. A hand lifted in a salute and he had turned away and was moving towards the other side of the street.

Staring after him, she told herself she was imagining all manner of ridiculous things, and all because of that look of secret amusement in his eyes. But she had no reason to be concerned on that score, for hadn't she managed to persuade the boss that she had no intention of allowing him to foot the bill for her special 'entertainment dress'? Feeling all at once happy and carefree, she made up her mind that she would buy a dress only if she found one that was the right price and exactly what she needed for the wine festival and any future engagements she might have at Sunvalley.

Willing herself not to be side-tracked by the fascinating stores she was passing, Sarah paused at last outside a small salon with the name 'Anton's' splashed in gold lettering across the window. She stepped inside the salon, but her cursory glance at the garments yielded nothing of interest. Nor did she fare any better in a spacious, well-stocked store featuring women's clothing.

Heavens, she thought, she wasn't having much success in her search. If she didn't find a dress she fancied at the boutique she was approaching...

It was a small, unpretentious room with little to choose from among the handful of dresses hanging from a long silver rod. The assistant, a pleasant-faced middle-aged woman who looked as if she had been poured into her perfectly fitting dark dress, greeted Sarah with a friendly smile. In a perceptive glance she took in Sarah's slim young figure and fair complexion, listening carefully as her customer explained the type of garment she was searching for.

Without wasting time the woman went into a back room, to return carrying over her arm a crimson dress, cleverly cut, distinctive and eye-catching. 'A little daring, maybe——' she held up the garment for Sarah's judgement '—but for an entertainer...'

Sarah, surveying the garment dubiously, shook her head. 'No, it's not what I want.'

She slung her bag over her shoulder and was about to turn away when the saleswoman's voice halted her. 'Wait! I happen to have a few garments that have never been picked up by customers who paid a deposit on them at the beginning of the summer. They're heavily reduced in price, a real bargain for anyone they happen to fit.'

She pulled aside a curtain in a corner of the salon, exposing a rainbow of coloured dresses on hangers. One garment, a soft black dress made of some filmy material, swayed gently in the breeze blowing in from the open window. Sarah liked it at sight, her swift glance taking in the attractive neckline, the slim, waist-hugging bodice and soft flounces falling from a dropped hipline.

It appeared to be her size, and the length seemed right for her too.

Before she could select the garment from the colourful array, however, a lean, sun-bronzed hand reached across her and deftly took the filmy dark dress from its hanger.

'How about this?' drawled an all-too-familiar masculine voice, and she swung around to meet Nick's glowing gaze. Wouldn't you know, she thought resentfully, that he would arrive at their meeting place ahead of time and trail her here at a moment when she could have wished him a thousand miles away?

Confusedly she realised that his appraising gaze was taking in the curves of her slender form, and for no reason at all she was finding difficulty in meeting his smiling glance. 'Bang on!' he was saying enthusiastically. 'Made for you and a perfect fit. You'll see!'

'I doubt it,' she lied.

As always there was no arguing with him. 'Try it on!' He tossed the filmy net garment over her arm.

Sarah's lips tightened mutinously. With any other man, she thought hotly, the words would have been a mere suggestion. With Nick they became more in the nature of a command!

But she was determined not to allow him to overrule her. Wasn't that the whole purpose of their making this trip to the city today, to enable her to choose her own dress to wear on the festival day?

Forcing her voice to the most nonchalant tone she could muster, she murmured, 'I'll think about it. I'll take this one too.' Wildly she jerked the dress nearest to her from the rail and marched into the fitting-room. She supposed she would have to try on the black dress. A suspicion niggled at the back of her mind that it would prove to be just the one she had hoped to find—subtle, soft, simple yet sophisticated. And hopefully, she told herself fiercely, it won't fit me! But it did, perfectly, delightfully. She surveyed her reflection in the long gilt-edged mirror, the soft black filmy net, soft as a breeze, whispering around her ankles. Why had she not worn black before? She hadn't thought it suited her in the past, but this dress was different, subtly complementing her pale skin and the slim curves of her figure. There was no doubt about it—this was her dress!

The price ticket when she looked at it made her blink. If this was bargain priced... But for once in her life, she thought recklessly, she was going to splash out and buy something she really wanted, whatever the cost. After all, she had funds as yet scarcely touched, and her wages from the vineyard would be coming in each week.

'Can I come in?' Nick's richly masculine voice cut across her moment of indecision.

For answer she jerked aside the curtain to meet his deep appreciative gaze. 'I like it!' His expression of satisfaction and pleasure was maddening. Anyone would imagine, Sarah thought crossly, that he had designed the dress himself. Flinging a glance towards the saleswoman, who was hovering in the background, he said jubilantly, 'That's it! That's the one! We'll take it!'

'*We*?' Sarah glared fiercely up into his animated face.

The saleswoman glanced uncertainly from Nick to Sarah. 'Madam is happy about the dress,' she enquired smoothly of Sarah, 'and the price?'

Once again a flood of anger threatened to submerge her. The curtain rings clattered together as with an angry jerk she pulled the curtain across until only her head was visible. 'Madam can make up her own mind!' she snapped. 'And yes——' she directed a furious glance in Nick's direction '—I suppose it will have to do!'

It seemed an age until at last she emerged from the cubicle, hair tousled every which way and her knitted primrose-coloured dress dragged on any old how.

To her relief the assistant was still writing out the docket.

'I'll pay for it.' Sarah was acutely aware of Nick standing at the counter, his mocking gaze taking in her flushed cheeks and dishevelled appearance. She dived into her shoulder-bag. 'I've come out here from England and I've only got traveller's cheques with me. Will that be all right?'

'Of course.'

She was still scrabbling in the contents of her bag. 'I know I've got them here...somewhere.' With hands that were not quite steady she rifled wildly through the contents. 'At least, I thought I had.' But she hadn't got them with her, she realised the next moment. In a sickening flash she remembered having taken the folder from her bag last night, and she couldn't have replaced it.

'I'm sorry,' she muttered unhappily to the waiting assistant, 'but I won't be able to take the dress after all.'

'It's OK.' Nick's smooth tones did nothing to lessen her mortification. He was placing a credit card on the counter, and Sarah waited in silence, her eyes shooting sparks at him as the woman wrote out the receipt.

Wrapping the dress in tissue paper, she placed it in a gold and white plastic bag and handed it to Nick. As he bade her goodbye the woman's smile included Sarah. 'I hope you'll come again.'

4
Free!
Plus a Free
Teddy &
Mystery Gift!

Temptation romances

In heartbreak and in ecstasy Temptations capture all the bittersweet joys of contemporary romance.

And to introduce to you this powerful and fulfiling series, we'll send you ***4 Temptation romances*** absolutely **FREE** when you complete and return this card.

We're so confident that you'll enjoy Temptations that we'll also reserve a subscription for you, to our Reader Service, which means that you could enjoy...

- **4 BRAND NEW TEMPTATIONS** - sent direct to you each month (before they're available in the shops).
- **FREE POSTAGE AND PACKING** - we pay all the extras.
- **FREE MONTHLY NEWSLETTER** - packed with special offers, competitions, author news and much more...

Free Books and Gifts claim

Yes Please send me my 4 FREE Temptation romances together with my FREE gifts. Please also reserve a special Reader Service subscription for me. If I decide to subscribe, I will receive 4 superb new Temptations for just £7.00 every month, post and packing FREE. If I decide not to subscribe I shall write to you within 10 days. The FREE books and gifts will be mine to keep. I understand that I am under no obligation whatsoever. I may cancel or suspend my subscription at any time simply by writing to you. I am over 18 years of age.

.1A3T

Name ______________________

Address ______________________

____

______________ **Postcode** ______________

Signature ______________________

Offer expires 30th April 1993. One per household. The right is reserved to refuse an application and change the terms of this offer. Readers overseas and Eire, send for details. Southern Africa write to: Book Services International Ltd. P.O. Box 41654 Craighall Transvaal 2024. You may be mailed with offers from other reputable companies as a result of this application. If you would prefer not to share in this opportunity, please tick box ☐

Association of Mail Order Publishers — mps MAILING PREFERENCE SERVICE

NO STAMP NEEDED

Mills & Boon Reader Service
FREEPOST
P.O. Box 236
Croydon
CR9 9EL

Send NO money now

'Not if I can help it!' Sarah said under her breath, and went with flaming cheeks to walk at Nick's side as they moved out into the city's main street.

'Don't be like that,' Nick said in the heart-catching voice that, in spite of everything, could still do things to her traitorous emotions. 'It's all part of the act. I don't know what you're getting so het up about.' Sarah's swift upward glance took in the mocking twist to the edges of his lips and she realised that he understood all too well her feelings on the matter.

'I wouldn't have taken it,' she said spiritedly. 'Not until I had the money to pay for it! I'd have come back with the money...somehow.'

'You wouldn't, you know.' They had reached the Land Rover and he was unlocking the doors. 'You wouldn't have been able to get here. Right! You've guessed it!' He caught her angry glance. 'I wouldn't have brought you back to town tomorrow.'

'I wouldn't have asked you!' Suddenly a thought crossed her mind. 'Would *you* take traveller's cheques?' she asked.

He said quietly, 'Not from you, Sarah.'

But she wasn't beaten yet. 'Then you'll have to take the cost of the dress out of my wages!' she said stormily, climbing up the high step of the Land Rover. 'And I don't care if it takes every cent I earn.'

Nick closed the heavy door of the vehicle, then went round to climb into the driver's seat, and turned towards her. 'Now get this straight! The entertainment at Sunvalley is something I pay for, it goes without saying. You've seen the records of last year's expenses?'

'Yes, I have! And they didn't include Darren's gear that he wore that day of the wine festival! Or the traditional frock worn by the girl who accompanied him on the guitar. It was just a straight fee covering the engagement.' To her chagrin her voice wobbled. 'I've told and told you, but you don't seem to understand. 'I don't *need* you to buy me things. As I said, *I'll* pay for the dress out of my wages!'

He shrugged broad shoulders. 'Fair enough, if that's what you want,' he said, and spoiled her moment of victory by adding offhandedly, 'I'll raise your pay accordingly, of course.'

Sarah opened her lips in protest, then closed them again. Oh, he made her so mad! Arrogant, self-opinionated, there was just no way of getting the better of him.

A wry smile twisted her lips, and of course his perceptive gaze didn't miss her expression. 'What's so funny?' he demanded.

She said very low, 'Nothing, nothing. It's just that I was thinking how horribly stubborn you can be once you've made up your mind about anything.'

Nick slanted her an ironical glance. 'Funny, I was thinking just the same thing about you. "Pigheaded" is the Kiwi word for it,' he added, and reached out a hand to put the vehicle into gear.

They moved down the colourful street with its shimmering mirror-glass façades and attractive display windows just as though, Sarah thought heatedly, there had been no arguments, no angry discussion between them.

'Swags of stores in this area,' Nick was saying equably. 'If you'd care to take a look around I could pick you up later.'

'No, thanks,' she said coldly. Without money in her bag even window-shopping had lost its allure, and she'd die, she'd just die, before she would ask him for a loan today.

'I didn't think you would,' he drawled.

Heartless brute!

CHAPTER SIX

EVEN as she let herself into the cottage Sarah was still seething with resentment against her employer. Hurrying into the bedroom, she dumped the black dress in its plastic bag on the bed and went into the kitchen to take chilled orange juice from the fridge.

Feeling strangely restless, she picked up a magazine, scanned the headlines, then tossed it aside. She seemed unable to concentrate on the printed words. Was it because Nick's enigmatic features rose on the screen of her mind?

At last she picked up the guitar Nick had brought her, her strong fingers plucking softly at the strings. Here was her opportunity to go over her repertoire of ballads and popular melodies in readiness for the wine festival only two days ahead.

First of all, though, just for fun, she would try out the New Zealand folk-song that Nick set such store by. Not that she would ever play it in public, of course. She was just curious. Leaping to her feet, she hurried into the bedroom and, picking up her jeans, fished the musical score from the pocket. She smoothed out the crumpled paper and soon she was bent low over the guitar, a lock of thick brown hair falling over her forehead as slowly she picked out the melody. It wasn't long before the throbbing notes fell into a rhythm, and with one foot tapping to the insistent beat she sent the rousing chorus flooding out into the still air. As she had suspected, it was the melody she had heard Nick whistling as he went about his duties in the vineyard.

Suddenly she laid down the instrument and, impelled by an urge she had been trying to resist all evening, she went to her wardrobe and riffled through the dresses hanging there. Mere curiosity, of course, she told herself, but she might as well take a look at the traditional Yugoslav costume that Nick was so enthusiastic about, darn him! That was, if she could find it. She flung open a drawer at the foot of the wardrobe and found a screwed-up bundle of material. She drew it out and found herself looking at a long dress of gossamer cotton with full sleeves and flowing hemline heavy with exquisite hand-embroidery in shades of cream and rose. She drew the soft folds over her head and, glancing in the long mirror, had to admit that the European-style dress did a lot for her. But that wasn't the point, she told herself sternly; it was the principle that mattered. Attractive though it was, she wouldn't ever wear it. She dragged the dress over her head, rolled it roughly into a bundle and hurled it back into the darkest corner of the cupboard. There! So far as she was concerned it could stay there for ever!

That night the humidity in the air was intense. Lying in bed, Sarah tossed and turned endlessly as long peals of thunder rolled over the hills and she waited for the flashes of lightning that followed. All at once thunder crashed so loudly that she felt sure it must be right above her head. She had never experienced an electrical storm such as this. If only the rain would come it would cool the atmosphere.

At last abandoning all hope of getting to sleep, she decided to cool off down in the pool. The prospect of dropping into the water was enticing, and it took her only a moment or two to slip into her black bikini.

Outside she felt the touch of dew-wet grass on her bare feet. The air was heavy with the threat of impending rain, trees a dark tracery against a brooding sky. Lightning played endlessly over the shadowy waters of the pool.

The touch of wind-ruffled water was bliss, and Sarah swam the length of the pool, her clean, swift strokes making scarcely a ripple as she went on. When she reached the end of the pool she paused, feeling her feet on a firm surface. She pushed streaming wet hair back from her forehead and was about to turn when a shadow darker than the rest moved. 'Hi, Sarah!' came Nick's mocking drawl.

'You!' Her stupid heart missed a beat and a quiver ran through her senses. She heard herself rushing into speech, saying inanely, 'What are *you* doing here?'

He said calmly, 'Just cooling off.'

'At three in the morning?'

'Look who's talking——' A peal of thunder drowned his words. 'Race you to the end of the pool,' he said. Lightning played for a moment over a black sky, illuminating his laughing face.

She had turned in a flash and was striking out over the dark water, but she didn't stand a chance, she realised at once, in competition with Nick's easy crawl. He was waiting for her when her feet touched the hard surface of the pool, a dark shadow among the overhanging bushes.

An instinct of danger made her say breathlessly, 'I'm going in——'

He moved through the water, barring her way. 'What's the hurry?'

Nothing threatening in his tone, so why did she have this fast-beating heart? Swiftly she turned aside. 'See you in the morning.'

His firm clasp on her wet arm halted her. 'You're trembling.' There was an unaccustomed cadence in his low tone. 'Why are you trembling, Sarah?'

'Cold.' She was breathing fast. 'I'm cold.'

'I'd let you go if that were true.' He was still retaining his firm grip on her arm. 'Why are you running away?'

'I'm not running away!' she flashed back. 'How can I when you won't let me go? Do you know,' she heard herself chattering on with the first words that entered her head, anything to break the dangerous spell of his nearness she could feel ensnaring her senses more deeply with each passing moment, 'when I first caught sight of you here in the pool tonight I thought you'd followed me from the cottage——?'

'*Followed you*?' She hated him when he spoke to her in that cool, mocking tone. 'Why would I do that?' he asked.

'How should I know?' His touch on her arm was sending her thoughts into turmoil. 'I guess because you wanted me to tell you I'll sing that special song of yours at the festival.'

'It sounded pretty good to me when you went over it this afternoon; should sound even better at the festival——'

So he had overheard her playing the melody today. The arrogance of the man! She was trying to keep control of her temper. He actually imagined she would leap to do his bidding even though she had told him she had no intention of singing the song! 'No!' she flung at him. 'I told you! I won't sing it—ever!'

'No?' The silence was heavy with meaning. At last Nick said, very low, 'I could make you change your mind.'

Something in the disturbing timbre of his voice, potent as a caress, sent her senses spinning in confusion. Her breath was coming unevenly, but she was determined not to allow him to guess at her feelings. Let him advance any arguments he could think of; he didn't stand a chance of influencing her. 'Try me!' she taunted in a voice bright with challenge, and waited for his fresh line of persuasion.

Before she could guess his intention, however, he caught her close. She could feel his hard, sinewy chest pressed against her slender body, stiff and resistant. The next moment his lips, damp with water, came down on hers in a passionate and lingering kiss. Then she ceased to struggle in his grasp, for beneath the pressure of his lips wave after wave of fiery sweetness was coursing its way through her and feelings she had never before experienced took over. The electricity-laden air seemed to charge her body with a life force there was no resisting, and time ceased to matter.

At last Nick released her. She caught his low, exultant laugh and his husky tones reached her through the darkness. 'I told you I could make you change your mind.'

It took a moment or two for the import of his words to register in her bemused mind, then realisation came with chilling force.

'You—you——' Her throat thickened and her voice died into silence. Fool that she was, she had totally misinterpreted the huskiness of his tones, his low, triumphant laughter. It was all just a trick, a deliberate play on her emotions to persuade her to sing his wretched song. And the humiliating part of it all was that she had responded ardently to his caress.

All at once a fierce anger mushroomed up inside her to explode in accusing words. 'Well, I've got news for you!' she flung at him. 'I haven't changed my mind, and I never will!'

She flung around and swam away from him, her clean strokes taking her swiftly to the other end of the pool. This time he made no attempt to detain her. Why should he? she thought hotly. Even Nick, stubborn and deceitful as she knew him to be, must know when he was beaten.

Hating herself, hating Nick, she climbed out of the pool, water streaming from her hair as she ran over the dew-wet grass back to the cottage, away from the power he so effortlessly exerted over her wayward emotions. How could she have forgotten, she raged inwardly, the type of man he really was? A wave of pain clutched her heart. And she had actually imagined he had kissed her because he—wanted to. How crazy could you get? Sick with humiliation and anger, she stumbled inside.

In the bright morning light she awoke feeling listless and heavy-eyed. But she was determined that Nick would never guess at her real feelings for him. He was away from the vineyard all day, however, and she told herself that that suited her just fine. Not that he would care about her one way or the other. His disturbing kiss that had cost her a night's sleep and shaken her world had been nothing to him. If only she could regard it in the same way.

On the following day she told herself that, among the crowd of visitors expected at the wine festival, she would see little of Nick, and anyway she would be busy entertaining the guests. What you need, girl, she told herself briskly, is work, anything to make you forget. And what better way to lose herself in the job in hand than to clean up the bottle store before the arrival of the crowd of visitors expected later in the day?

As she made her way along the path to the bottle store she could see that, early though it was, Nick was setting out small tables and seats in the shade of the giant macrocarpa trees and putting up trestle-tables not far from the barbecue area. There was no avoiding him so, drawing a deep breath, she threw him a cool nod, forcing her voice to a nonchalant note. 'Morning, Nick!'

'Hi, Sarah!' He sent her a smile that all but wrecked her intentions of putting him right out of her mind. 'All set for the big day?'

'I guess so,' she murmured offhandedly, and hurried away.

When she reached the kitchen in the house Kate greeted her with relief. 'Come in, Sarah, you're just in time. I was going to come and find you——' She gave a harassed glance around the room, where every inch of available space was taken up with crockery and foodstuffs, freshly picked lettuce, onions, cooked potatoes, stacks of various cheeses, bowls of dips and a variety of small bite-sized canapés. 'If you could just help me with the salads,' Kate told her. 'I like to provide a good variety to go with the steaks Nick barbecues.'

Soon Sarah was busily engaged in the various tasks, and time passed swiftly as benches and table were covered in great bowls holding luscious varieties of salads together with sauces, dishes of salad dressings, cooked mushrooms, tiny zucchini. To Sarah there seemed no end to the variety of food provided for the barbecue meal to be held later in the day.

'If you could take out the plates and cutlery from the box,' Kate suggested, 'and put it all in piles on the trestle-table by the barbecue so folk can help themselves. Oh, and put out the bites and chips and nuts on the tables, so they'll have something to nibble while they drink the wine that Nick puts out for them.'

Sarah had completed her tasks and was about to return to the cottage to grab a bite to eat and change into the black dress when Kate called her back. 'Wait! Just one more thing! I almost forgot! The notice board——'

'Notice board?' Sarah looked puzzled.

'Here it is.' Kate produced a large oblong of plywood together with drawing-pins. 'You'll need these,' she said, and handed Sarah a cardboard folder evidently containing newspaper clippings and photographs. 'We put the board out every year on festival day—all part of the proceedings, and it does provide a bit of interest of how the vineyard was started and all that.'

Obligingly Sarah tucked the folder beneath her arm and staggered outside with the board. Setting it against a tree-trunk, she kneeled on the grass and began to sort out clippings and pictures.

'Hey, let me give you a hand!' Startled, she glanced up to find Nick at her side. Surely she must be imagining the tiny points of light glowing in the depths of his dark eyes, for he was running on just as if there had been no emotional encounter between them on the night of the electrical storm. No doubt he had forgotten the incident, dismissing it from his mind as of no importance. She wrenched her mind back to his drawling tones.

'The family history pictures are part of the show.' He was bending over, selecting a black and white photograph from the pile of pictures and cuttings lying on the dried grass and pinning it to the board.

Sarah found herself gazing at a picture of a Mediterranean bay where fishing boats were moored at the water's edge and stone cottages dotted the steep slopes above.

'This is the island in the Adriatic Sea where it all began and the wine-making tradition was born. Here's Nikolo.' He held up a photograph of a dark-haired young man. 'He was a vintner by tradition and he left his island to come to a country about as far away as you could get from the family vineyard. The only work he could find in the new country was digging gum from under the kauri trees in the far north. It was tough going; the earth was rock-hard and the workers lived in rough huts. But he managed to save enough to buy a few acres here. The land and the climate were much the same as the island in the Adriatic he'd come from.'

He held out another picture of the same young dark-eyed man. 'Here he is grubbing gorse and blackberry from the land to make way for the European-style vineyard he planned. And look, here's the wedding picture. Zena was his childhood sweetheart back home where he came from.'

Interested in spite of herself, Sarah forgot her resentment towards Nick as she regarded the faded photograph. 'But the groom looks different——'

'Oh, he's not the bridegroom.' Nick's voice was careless. 'That's his brother Peter.'

'His brother!'

He grinned at her incredulous expression. 'Nikolo couldn't afford to get back to his own country, and it was difficult for her to get papers to come to New Zealand except as his wife, so they were married in a rush by proxy, Nikolo's brother standing in as Zena's bridegroom before she took the sea journey from Europe. They had a celebration in their wedding gear the day she arrived in the new country. Here they are together——'

Sarah's gaze swept the headline of the newspaper cutting—'THE SUN SHINES ON ZENA AND NICK'—then her attention moved to the dark-haired man and girl who were standing together under a frame of vines. Something about their look of shining happiness touched her. 'I wonder if she was lonely so far away from her own people?'

'She was lonely as hell. At first she didn't think she could stick it, but once they came to the valley she was determined to make a go of it.' The glint in his eyes mocked her. 'She was working alongside her man. It was the way she wanted it.'

Sarah raised her eyes heavenwards in exasperation. 'I know; you told me all about it.'

He ignored her comment. He would!

'Coming up three generations later——' he was selecting a studio photograph from the pile '—a distant, very distant relative of mine.' All at once the note of light-hearted gaiety died out of his tones. 'Steven. A great guy, one of the best. He used to run the vineyard here before I—took over.'

Sarah caught her breath. She recognised the portrait at once. Hadn't she seen the picture standing on her sister's bureau all those years ago in their London home right up to the day of the accident that had claimed Kathy's life?

She looked down at the bearded masculine face through a blur of tears. Steven, the way she remembered him—the thick black hair and trimmed dark beard, the kindly expression in his dark eyes. All at once she felt a surge of betrayal. What was she doing in the vineyard, a stranger who had inherited the property only through a twist of fate? Had she known the true position, realised the tradition belonging to Sunvalley, she would never have come here. But then, whispered a small imp deep in her mind, you would never have known Nick. She thrust it away. Wherever could that absurd thought have come from?

'Here's another shot of him——' Nick's voice broke across her musing '—taken somewhere in Europe. He took a trip over there to get a line on vineyards on the other side of the world.'

He picked up a snapshot from the pile of pictures lying on the grass beside him. 'You wouldn't be interested in this one—just a snap taken by an instamatic in a garden. A girl he got to know on his trip overseas.' Why did she get the feeling he was avoiding any reference to Kathy? 'You wouldn't be interested.' He made to toss the snapshot down on a pile of pictures he had discarded, but almost without her volition she had snatched it up. *Not interested*? Her heart gave a sickening lurch as she stared down at a once familiar scene on the other side of the world, the back yard of a brick house. Another part of her mind registered a passing red double-decker bus on the road outside.

She was aware only of the tall, bearded masculine figure, smiling, happy, his arm thrown around the waist of the slight girl who was nestling into his shoulder. With a stab of the heart she gazed down at a picture of Kathy, her sister, looking up at Steven with such love and happiness that it seemed to beam right out of the photo. Only then did she notice a girl of eight who was herself, standing shyly beside Kathy, her hand clasped in that of her sister.

The picture was worn and creased as though someone had carried it around in his pocket for a long time. Steven's most precious possession, maybe, this shot taken on her mother's little instamatic in the back yard of their London home so long ago? Now it was indisputable evidence of her crazy masquerade.

Did he suspect? She didn't dare look at Nick for fear he should guess her secret. She was hopeless at disguising her feelings, she'd been told often enough. At last she risked a swift upward glance, but his cool gaze gave nothing away. Surely if he doubted her identity, her reason for being here, he would flay her with hot, accusing words. She shuddered at the thought.

His drawling tones cut across her panicky musing. 'I thought you'd recognise where that picture was taken.'

Did he know? Her thoughts raced confusedly. Was he guessing, waiting for her to give herself away?

A resemblance must have betrayed her. Or had it? Her hair was fair in those days, tied back in a pony-tail. But all the same... She heard her own voice sounding curiously muffled. 'London, you mean?' At last her distraught mind shifted into top gear and inspiration came in the nick of time. It was worth a try. 'You mean the double-decker bus? In London they take tourists on tours around the city all the time.' Don't look at Nick, she told herself. 'Especially in—in the summer.' She was scarcely aware of what she was saying.

Suddenly there was a queer drumming in her ears and a dizzy feeling was stealing over her. His voice seemed to be coming from a distance. 'Are you feeling all right, Sarah?'

The sharp note of his deep tones was as bracing to her taut nerves as a dash of cold water. She pulled herself together and even managed a wobbly smile. 'Of course I am! Why shouldn't I be?'

'You've gone white all of a sudden——'

'Oh, that?' She tried to make her voice light and carefree. 'It's nothing, just something that happens to me now and again. It doesn't mean a thing.'

'Thank heaven for that!'

A great wave of relief flooded her. She had been sick with fear that he might have recognised her in the long-ago picture, but everything was all right after all. *He didn't know*. Clearly he hadn't the slightest suspicion of any link between herself and the fair-haired child in the snapshot. A great weight seemed to have lifted from her shoulders.

His sideways glance swept her young face, the sweetly curved lips, the flawless skin now tinged with faint colour. 'You're looking better already,' he said. If he only knew the reason for the pink that was returning to her pale cheeks.

Sarah was surprised and touched by his concern for her well-being. The next minute the penny dropped. But of course his solicitude was for the entertainer he had booked for the coming wine festival and whom he would have difficulty in replacing at short notice. What else?

Aloud she said, 'Don't worry, I won't let you down with the music at the last minute.'

His answer was an odd, unfathomable look that she couldn't interpret. But then there was no understanding him—ever.

Presently she hurried back to the cottage to take a quick shower and to wash her hair. The dark strands would dry in no time at all on this hot, sunshiny day. A hint of green eyeshadow to her eyelids and a touch of lip-gloss to her mouth completed her toilet. The gauzy black dress she found was a delight to wear. Already through the window she glimpsed the first visitors arriving. Picking up her guitar, she threaded her way through the chattering groups, scarcely noticed by the crowd of guests now thronging the grounds of the vineyard. She took up a stand beneath a shady tree and began testing the strings of her instrument.

'You look terrific!' Startled, she swung around. She hadn't been aware of Nick's approach, and here he was at her side, thickly lashed dark eyes deep and compelling as he surveyed her.

'Oh!' She moistened dry lips. 'The dress, you mean?'

'Not the dress.' At his appreciative gaze she could feel the tell-tale colour rising in her cheeks and forgot all about being cool and uncaring towards him.

'Hi, Nick!' A chorus of male voices called him away and, cheeks still flushed, Sarah bent over the guitar. They'll never hear me singing in all this noise, she thought, but anyway, here goes!

As the notes of the guitar throbbed through the clear air and her young voice, sweet and clear, rang out with surprising strength, talk and laughter died away and all eyes were on the slim girl standing alone, her dark head bent over the instrument.

'I'll sing and play what I please,' she had told the boss, and she intended to do just that. Beginning with a few old-timers, she went on to play a Country and Western melody, then, with scarcely a pause in the throbbing notes, she broke into the rhythm of a hit tune that was sweeping England at the time she left there and was evidently familiar to her audience on the other side of the world.

At last she paused and set the guitar down against the tree-trunk, her gaze roving the crowded scene. Nick was standing among a group of men, and at that second he glanced towards her. For an instant their glances meshed and held, then she looked away, forcing herself to concentrate on her musical programme.

A few minutes later she became aware that he was threading his way through the groups of guests. 'Come along, Sarah.' His dark eyes held a dancing light as he approached her.

Suddenly, for no reason at all, she was swept by a tide of happiness. Something to do, no doubt, with the sparkling day where bushes were sun-gilded and the sky above was a translucent blue. It's because of the inheritance, she told herself, my inheritance! Even if it's only temporary. A tiny voice whispered, deep down where it counted, *My man*! Absurd—she loathed Nick, remember? All this hot sunshine must be going to her head.

She brought her mind back to his rich tones. Why must he have a voice like that—deep, almost caressing? It was an effort to concentrate on his words. 'Highlight of the vintage party,' he explained, still with that air of contained excitement, 'the special wine-tasting ceremony for the new wine. The first bottle of the new vintage for everyone to taste. It's green, not even bottled yet and taken from the tank. So new that it hasn't got a name—any suggestions?'

Still under the spell, Sarah flashed him a mischievous smile.

'How about Happy Valley?'

'Why not?' There was an odd note in his tone. 'Come along, it's an occasion. Especially for you——'

She hesitated, eyeing him suspiciously. If this was his idea of a joke... Her glance moved and through a gap in the crowd she glimpsed a small table set with glasses and a single bottle of wine. Among the group she recognised familiar faces: the women pickers she had got to know at the harvesting of the grapes. Penny, the girl who lived next door on the kiwi-fruit plantation, her husband Bill and a youth who occasionally drove the truck for Nick. Nick said, 'They're waiting for you.'

'Me?' Her voice came out as an incredulous squeak. 'Why me, for heaven's sake? I haven't done anything!'

'You're one of us.' He looked happy and excited. 'Everyone's invited to the occasion—staff and anyone else who's been in any way concerned with the year's wine-making.'

Still she held back. 'I scarcely qualify. I've only been here a short time——'

'Listen!' Above the babble of talk and laughter voices rose in a chant of, 'Sarah! We want Sarah!'

'Coming!' Nick called back to the group, and, throwing an arm carelessly around her shoulders, he piloted her through the throng.

'You'll see wine-growers here today from all parts of the country,' he told her as they went on. She tried to concentrate on what he was telling her, but his touch was doing things to her emotions, sending a dizzy sweetness soaring through her. What was he saying? 'Here comes one from a lot further south, but it doesn't take him long to make the trip from the family sheep station.' She tried to fix her attention on a light plane that came soaring over the hills and dropped height to glide down on a grassy area near by. The tiny microlight plane resembled a gigantic pink insect. The next minute a masculine figure leaped down from the frail craft and, smiling and waving to the crowd, hurried towards Nick and Sarah.

CHAPTER SEVEN

'HI, NICK!' A lanky, loose-limbed young man with wind-tossed red hair caught up with them, and although he had called to Nick he couldn't seem to take his gaze from Sarah.

'Sarah,' Nick said briefly. 'Larry.'

'Hello, Larry.' She smiled in response to his warm grin. 'We had a chat over the phone the other day—your special invitation to the wine festival here, remember?' Could it be the masses of freckles scattered over his face and arms, she wondered, that lent him a boyish appearance?

He said very low, 'As if I could forget you! I've been looking forward all week to——' He broke off, a dark flush rising on his freckled cheeks. And, glancing from one man to the other, Sarah was surprised to notice Nick's dark, forbidding expression. 'I didn't know,' Larry murmured in evident confusion, 'that you and Nick——'

Nick said repressively, 'Sarah works for me at the vineyard.'

'That's right.' In an effort to ease his discomfiture Sarah flashed the unhappy young man a smile. After all, he had done nothing to merit Nick's displeasure. 'I'm here on a working holiday from England,' she told him, 'and I'm enjoying every minute of it.'

When they reached the wine-tasting table Nick, in one of his mercurial changes of mood, joked and talked with the crowd gathered round the table, his dark eyes sparkling with good humour and merriment.

Pouring a measure of wine into glasses, he waited until everyone had been served, then, amid a chorus of cheers and good wishes, he raised his glass. 'To Happy Valley.'

'To Happy Valley.' Glasses chinked together, and Sarah joined in the chorus of voices. The next moment she realised with surprise that the boss was gazing not around his cheering audience but directly towards her. She had been too much involved with her music to do more than taste the wine that had flowed so freely, so that wasn't the cause of the wild, sweet excitement she was feeling.

Blame the sparkling day or, more likely, she admitted to herself, Nick's charisma that, in spite of all she knew of him, worked its magic on her wayward heart. All at once common sense returned with a rush. For heaven's sake, she reminded herself, she had supplied him with a name for his new season's wine, hadn't she?

Presently she left the others to return to take up her position beneath the shady tree, and once again she picked up her guitar. Soon she had no time for pauses between numbers, for even a brief interval in her playing was greeted with applause followed by loud calls of, 'More! More!' From all but Nick. She caught glimpses of him apparently deep in conversation with groups of men whom she took to be wine-growers from other parts of the country who were here today to honour the new vintage.

As the hours wore on she continued her entertainment even though the crowd, now in high spirits, no longer paused to listen to her songs. Only Larry appeared to be interested in her playing. For although he spent brief periods renewing acquaintances he always returned to her side. She became accustomed to the sight of his tall figure approaching her, often a cool drink for her in his hand.

'Why don't you take a break?' His boyish tones held a note of entreaty.

Sarah laughed and shook her head, and as the notes died into silence she gave him a teasing smile. 'I do get paid for entertaining, you know.'

Much later, when an amethyst haze lay over the bush-covered hills, Sarah watched as willing helpers set out the plates of food that Kate had prepared on trestle-tables. Not far away smoke was rising from a barbecue. Sarah, however, was content to remain where she was and provide background music throughout the meal. At Larry's pleas for her to go with him and join the groups now moving towards the trestle-tables she shook her head, once again sending the dark brown hair flinging in a curtain across her cheeks. 'I'm not hungry,' she told him.

He turned away, a look of disappointment in his eyes. 'I'll wait for you there, then.'

'Maybe I'll join you later,' she called after him.

'You won't, you know,' drawled a familiar male voice, and she glanced up to find Nick at her side. 'Barbecue steaks are meant to be enjoyed right now, not an hour or so later!'

Sarah bent over the strings. 'I really don't want——'

'*Now!*' Strong hands loosened the instrument from her grasp and he tossed it down on the grass.

It was no use. 'You're the boss,' Sarah said resignedly, and allowed him to escort her through the crowd and in the direction of a food-laden table.

At the other end of the table a blond giant of a man rose to his feet, and Nick said easily, 'Kevin, this is Sarah.'

The stranger's blue eyes were warm with male interest. 'So you're the girl Nick took on for summer work in the vineyard!' Although appearing to be in his early twenties, he had a slow, deliberate manner of speech. 'The way Nick was talking about you, I might have known!'

Sarah's enquiring glance went to Nick's face. His tightened lips and smouldering dark eyes left no doubt in her mind that he was anything but pleased at the turn the conversation had taken. She thought wryly that, whatever it was Nick had told the big blond man about her, she would never know.

At that moment Nick took her arm and together they strolled towards the smoking barbecue. When they got back to the table Sarah made her selection from various salad dishes. The next moment she found Kevin at her side. He had a friendly smile and a pleasant face, she thought. 'How are you enjoying life out here, anyway? Nick's not working you too hard, is he?' His blue eyes twinkled.

'It's not the work——' Just in time she stopped herself from uttering the thoughts that clamoured in her mind. Instead she said, 'It's a great experience working in a vineyard.' She had no need to force the note of enthusiasm in her tones. 'Especially when the grapes are ripe in the New Zealand summer when everyone back home in England is shivering with the cold!' That at least was the truth. Her laughing gaze went to Larry, who had just joined them. 'And I've seen my first microlight plane!' She smiled up at Larry. 'I just couldn't believe it was real, it looked so frail, skimming over the hills. I'm going to ask him to take me up with him for a flight.'

'No need to ask!' Larry's freckled face had lighted up. 'Just make a day, and the sooner, the better. How about the weekend?'

Smilingly Sarah glanced around the table. 'Tell me, am I being brave about this or just stupid? Who cares? I'm going to take a flight anyway!'

'*No*!' Nick's explosive tone brooked no argument, and in the startled silence faces all around the table were turned towards him. The next minute a chorus of indignant voices rang out in protest. 'Don't be such a spoilsport, Nick! Let the girl have some fun!'

Sarah was aware of his deep, penetrating glance. 'Do you really want to go up in the microlight?' he asked her.

For a moment she hesitated, confused by the mesmeric influence of his intense dark stare, remembering her initial surprise that the frail-looking open craft could lift into the air, let alone take a passenger and land safely at its destination. The thoughts flew through her mind. If only it didn't put her in mind of a kit-set machine, all made of lengths of timber and pieces of aluminium strung together.

'I knew you'd be having second thoughts.'

At the satirical lift of Nick's well-cut lips perversely she went in the opposite direction. 'Well, I haven't!' She made an attempt to look unconcerned about the proposed flight. 'It'll be an experience,' she asserted with more confidence than she felt, 'something to write home about after the weekend.'

'Sorry.' Sarah thought Nick looked anything but regretful at putting an end to any arrangements she might have made in the matter of a flight. His bland glance went to Larry's downcast face. 'I've got a special job lined up for Sarah at the weekend. Last-minute labelling and packaging all that stuff, as well as a special tour party I'm half expecting then. I've found by experience that guitar music adds to the atmosphere of the place—and the overseas orders!'

Sarah opened her mouth to speak, then closed it again. For once in her life she was speechless. She glared up at him. How dared he interfere in her personal affairs? The thoughts rushed through her mind. Could he be getting back at her because of her refusal to do his bidding in the matter of entertainment today? Surely he didn't have work for her to do at the weekend that was as urgent as all that? But it seemed that that was exactly what he did have—or so he said. 'Sarah can take time off later,' he said carelessly.

A silence had fallen over the group that had been chattering and laughing around the table. Larry's face had fallen, but he seemed to get the message that when it came to arrangements concerning his Girl Friday, even at weekends, the boss meant business. However, he managed a fairly cheerful reply. 'Guess it will have to be some other time, then.'

A little later Nick left the group to go into the reception-room to attend to stereo music, and soon the foot-tapping beat of a popular dance hit drowned the laughter and chatter around them. Larry laid a hand on Sarah's arm. 'Gotta go,' he ground out on a sigh, 'worse luck.'

'What do you mean?' she asked, puzzled.

'Take a look over there!' She followed his gaze to the setting sun now sinking in a ball of fire that painted the western horizon in long rays of flame and orange.

'It's not all fun and games piloting a microlight,' he told her ruefully. 'I've got to be on my way before dark. Look.' All at once his low tones were tinged with urgency. 'I will see you again, won't I?' Before she could answer he went on, 'There's something——' he clasped her hands in his warm grip '—you won't mind my asking you? It's just——' Nervously he licked dry lips. 'I mean,' he went on in a sudden rush of words, 'there's nothing going with you and Nick—is there?' His tone had a curious intensity. 'I wouldn't like to butt in. You know what I'm getting at?'

'Nick?' Sarah burst out incredulously. 'He's my boss, that's all. I scarcely know him!'

'I get it.' A relieved expression spread over Larry's freckled features. 'I'll see you again soon?'

'If you like.'

'Great!' He looked delighted. 'Believe me,' he told her in his candid way, 'I wouldn't leave you at all if I had my way. It wouldn't be so bad if I was going to see you at the weekend.' He gave a deep sigh. 'But seems the boss can't spare you, and I guess what he says goes.' All at once his tone deepened. 'You'll let me know if anything changes, if you can get away at the weekend? Just give me a buzz. Kate has the phone number and I'll be here to pick you up before you know it. We'll take a flight—you have no idea how great the countryside looks from way up there. Mountains look like mounds and sheep and cattle in fenced paddocks are dots.' He pressed her hand. 'You'll see.' His voice was very low.

'Promise me you'll try to make it, that you'll get in touch with me if there's a chance——'

'All right, then.' But she knew the chances of the boss changing his mind and allowing her time off at the weekend weren't worth considering. Not that she minded one way or the other. What she did mind was Nick's maddening authoritative attitude towards her. But she would get her own back for the way he had treated her today, she vowed, just see if she wouldn't!

''Night, Sarah! Hate to have to leave you.'

She scarcely heard the low words, for from a corner of her eye she was aware of Nick standing not far away among a group of guests and taking in the little scene. On an impulse, and just to make certain he realised that she wasn't unattractive to other men, she raised her face to Larry's, and said softly, 'Goodnight.' His lips brushed hers in a gentle kiss.

'See you,' he tossed back gruffly over his shoulder as he turned away and almost at once was lost to sight among the crowd.

'Dance, Sarah?'

She glanced up to find Kevin towering over her. Swiftly she gathered her thoughts together and summoned a bright smile. 'Why not?' Soon they were moving among other couples beneath the soft glimmer of the fairy lights strung overhead.

'Do you know,' she murmured, 'I was dancing to this song just before I left England to come out here? You *are* up to date with things.'

'Where did you hear it?' asked Kevin.

'It was at a private party, a friend's twenty-first, actually.' Her thoughts drifted. Ridiculous to realise she would much rather be here in this valley, miles from anywhere, dancing on the summer-dry grass in the shadows of the surrounding hills, than anywhere else, even with good friends back home. Strange that she felt so happy here, so much at home—except for Nick. Don't think of Nick. He's too possessive, too—disturbing. From somewhere deep down where it counted a voice whispered, And devastatingly attractive. Masculine charisma, call it what you liked, a force so powerful that you couldn't help but be aware of him when he was in the same room. And his aura of power and authority! Wasn't there a Maori word for it? *Mana*. Enigmatic, changeable, a man you either hated at sight or could fall deeply in love with. For herself, she hated him!

When the soft darkness fell they strolled towards the crowded reception-room where stereo music pulsed out through wide-open doors into the night. Kevin proved to be an outstanding dancer, his feet performing intricate steps on the polished floor with effortless ease. He claimed Sarah as a partner dance after dance, and that, she told herself, was fine with her. The last thing she wanted tonight was to be partnered by Nick—except, she reminded herself crossly, that dancing with him would provide an opportunity to let him know in no uncertain terms just how she felt about his high-handed, interfering tactics towards one of his staff.

She need not have concerned herself, however, she realised later in the evening, for he made no appearance on the dance-floor. She gave herself a mental shake. Why on earth was she thinking of *him* all the time anyway?

A long time later, when guests were moving towards cars, trucks and Land Rovers, Kevin was one of the last to leave.

When Sarah went into the house she found a cheerful group in the kitchen. Kate was busy at the sink, spraying detergent into steaming water, while Penny was stacking plates and dishes. Two local women were dealing with left-overs on plates and a youth she had noticed helping Nick grilling steaks at the barbecue earlier in the day was busy with a broom.

'Hi!' she greeted him, liking the boy at sight. He appeared to be about fifteen years of age, his legs encased in tight-fitting stone-washed jeans, and a cocky grin on his young face.

'This is Paul,' Kate called, turning towards Sarah from her task at the sink. 'He's one of the family, but his people live way down in the South Island, so we don't see much of him.'

The youth grinned. 'You will now, Aunt Kate! I can't wait to tell you the great news! Just wait until my mum hears about this!'

There was a sudden hush in the room. 'Nick says he'll take me on at the vineyard here for the summer, until I start varsity.' His eyes were sparkling with excitement. 'And what do you know? I'm taking chemistry as a subject, and Nick says it might come in useful to me in a few years. He might even take me on in the wine-making line with him if I work hard.' He gave a cocky grin. 'You never know your luck! He says I've got to stick to the grind, though, really pull my weight and all that—no slacking. I have to get the grades, he says, or it's not on. Now I've got an incentive to get through the years of slog, I'll show him what I can do! Nick, he's the sort of guy my mates would give their eye-teeth for when it comes to a holiday job. Straight from the shoulder, no messing about. If Nick says a thing—boy, he means it!'

You can say that again, Sarah agreed silently. Picking up a tea-towel, she wrenched her mind back to Paul's excited young tones.

'Nick says I'll have to toe the line, pick up all the gen I can about wine-making these holidays. Am I glad I got my driving licence! I can give him a hand with deliveries and all that. He says I can make myself useful in other directions too, like labelling, washing wine bottles, the lot—even put in some time in the bottle store. I just can't wait to get started tomorrow!'

Tomorrow! Sarah felt an icy shiver run down her spine. The bottle store, labelling... She too held an international driving licence, but Nick hadn't asked her about it, so she hadn't mentioned the matter. Did this mean that the youth—one of the family—had been given her job at the vineyard? Had she really gone too far in defying the autocratic orders of the boss? It was all too likely that he was about to replace her with this boy, eager to learn the wine trade, hero-worshipping Nick whom he had only met at rare intervals and didn't really know at all. He had been furiously angry with her on more than one occasion, but this... Suddenly she was swept by a sick feeling of emptiness and loss.

'You must be in love!' She became aware of Penny's laughing face. 'You've dried that salad bowl three times. If that's the effect Kevin has on you——'

'You look all in.' Kate's sharp glance was taking in Sarah's look of strain. 'You've been working all day while the rest of us have been enjoying ourselves——'

Swiftly Sarah rallied her sinking spirits. 'Oh, but I've been enjoying myself too! It's great to be able to help with the entertainment while I'm here——' She broke off, for Nick was standing in the open doorway and no doubt he was registering with satisfaction her last words. That was the moment when she panicked. With a low murmur, she told them, 'I think I'll call it a day!' and tossed down the towel and fled. For one dreadful moment she thought Nick was about to impede her progress, but he merely moved aside as she hurried past him out into the soft darkness of the night.

She had all but reached the cottage when she felt a touch on her arm and Nick, his footsteps silent on the dew-wet grass, fell into step at her side.

'You can sure make that guitar sing!' His vibrant tones rang with enthusiasm. 'Ever thought of taking up music as a career?'

The last thing she would have expected of him was glowing appreciation of her day's entertainment work, yet he actually seemed to mean it. If he could ignore everything else, she thought fiercely, so could she! She forced her voice to a nonchalant note. 'Not really. I've never had the time or the money for serious study along those lines!'

'You should! You're a natural!'

They had reached the cottage, and in the small outside porch she turned to face him. 'Glad you enjoyed it!' A flurry of confusion was sending her thoughts into a wild tumult. She took a deep breath. 'You've no complaints, then?'

'Just one thing——' He took a step nearer to her, much too close for the sudden thump-thump of her stupid heart. 'Tell me, did Larry make a date with you for a flight?' His drawling tones were as lazy as ever, so why did she get this impression of a loaded question?

'Larry?' She played for time. Then all at once she saw her opportunity to even the score with him and seized it. 'Oh, yes! He's going to arrange a day for me to go up with him in that funny little light plane of his.'

'Don't go!' His tone was so peremptory even for him that Sarah stared up at him in surprise. Really, of all the nerve! She lifted her small square chin challengingly. It was time he was taught a lesson!

'Why ever not?' she flung at him, and reached a hand towards the doorknob, but he stepped forward, barring her way. 'I told Larry I'd love to take a flight with him.' With assumed carelessness she added, 'I'm looking forward to it!' Actually she hadn't given the matter a second thought. 'If it's the danger bit that's on your mind,' she informed him triumphantly, 'you can forget it! Larry happens to have a pretty good track record! Me, I'm not in the least bit concerned!'

'But I am!' he ground out savagely. 'Now get this straight! You're not going up in that microlight with him. Not now, not ever!'

'For heaven's sake,' she said huffily, 'why ever not?'

'I won't have it!'

'*You* won't!' All the built-up resentment she felt towards him exploded in a rush of words. 'As I told you, I do as I please about my music—and my friends!' Because his silence was somehow more intimidating than the sarcastic retort she had expected from his lips she added defiantly, 'I only work here, you know! You don't own me!' Red danger flags rose in her cheeks. 'Anyway——' she eyed him suspiciously '—why did you tell Larry you couldn't spare me from the vineyard this weekend?'

'You heard me,' he said blandly. 'Pressure of business.' She didn't trust the flicker of triumph in his drawling tones one little bit.

'I wonder. You know something?' She couldn't seem to stop the flow of angry words that were spilling from her lips. 'I'd like to know just what you've got against Larry. He seemed quite nice to me——'

'Oh, sure, he's a nice guy!'

'Well, then?' Sarah looked at him suspiciously.

'Part of our agreement when you took the job here, remember?' Once again she caught the mocking tone in his voice. 'Something might come up at the weekend——'

'Might!' Suddenly she threw common sense to the wind. 'You're still mad with me just because I refused to play your special song today, alter my programme of music just to suit you!' She glared at him, her eyes shooting sparks.

Nick shrugged. 'I can wait——'

'Wait! How can you say that,' she flung at him, 'after—after——' to her horror her voice cracked '—what you did to me today?'

His voice was dangerously quiet. 'What's that supposed to mean?'

'As if you didn't know,' she said thickly, holding back tears that pricked her eyelids. All at once hurt and indignation gave way to hot anger. 'I had a chat with Paul tonight. He was all taken up with the job you've given him for the summer—*my* job!' Her voice throbbed accusingly. 'How could you do a thing like that?' She gritted her teeth to stop the sudden onslaught of tears. 'And you don't even care!'

He said very low, 'Who told you I'd given Paul your job?'

Without warning the effects of the long day, the sense of betrayal and loss overwhelmed her, and with the backs of her hands she dashed away the tears that trickled down her cheeks. 'Well, no one. I just thought——' Wildly she stumbled on, 'I mean, if it was someone with a current driver's licence you wanted, I've got that with me. I didn't tell you because I didn't think you'd be interested——'

'Not interested? In *you*, Sarah?' The sudden warmth in his husky tones took her by surprise, but the next moment his voice was as impersonal as ever, and she told herself she must surely have imagined that unexpected tenderness. Tenderness towards *her*? Nick? She must be out of her mind!

She wrenched her mind back to the present, trying to concentrate on what he was saying. 'You must have got your lines crossed. You've got it all wrong. Believe me, I can do with all the help I can get!'

'Oh.' She let out her breath on a sigh of relief. 'I thought you didn't want me.'

'Didn't want you, Sarah?' The muttered words were so low that she barely caught them, and the next moment she told herself she must have imagined them too. Tonight she seemed to be dreaming up all manner of wild assumptions, like emotional nuances in Nick's low tones and being forced to leave the vineyard right away because there was no longer any work for her here.

'Everything sorted out now?' His drawling tones cut across her musing.

'Oh, yes! Yes!' she assured him happily, and waited for him to tell her that he had no objection after all to her taking a flight with Larry in his microlight. Instead he muttered something unintelligible, then, ''Night, Sarah!' He turned sharply, and, moving with his long, leisurely stride, was swallowed up in the darkness.

'Have you seen Nick this morning?' Sarah glanced up from her office desk as Paul came into the room. 'I've got a phone message for him——'

'He took off with a girl—Lynn, he called her—ages ago. Said he wouldn't be back until tonight. She picked him up in her car first thing this morning. Wow-ee! Is she ever a looker! Blonde and beautiful as they come! Nick sure knows how to pick them!'

Sarah couldn't understand her sudden feeling of let-down. Hadn't she been told of the on-and-off relationship between her employer and his long-time love? It wasn't as if Nick meant anything to her—how could he? The reason she was feeling frustrated and angry, of course, was his taking off today, on the weekend he had forbidden her to leave the vineyard for a flight with Larry. Aloud she said, 'He didn't leave any message for me?'

'Not a word.'

A wave of resentment washed over her.

'I guess that leaves you and me in charge,' Paul was saying with an air of importance. 'It's OK with me. I'm happy here, and there's nowhere for you to go, not without transport.'

Sarah was scarcely aware of the boyish tones. All very well for Nick to leave her to cope with possible tour parties arriving at the vineyard in his absence. He had allowed her no choice in the matter, not even any special instructions. No doubt he had been too excited at the unexpected meeting with the girl he still loved to consider anyone else. Her soft lips firmed. Right! It was a game two could play! She glanced towards the window. A clear, windless day, the sky a brilliant blue. The perfect day for a microlight flight. And why not? She didn't *have* to do as Nick ordered her, she told herself defiantly. And if her absence from the vineyard cost him important new clients, it was his own fault!

The next minute she was picking up the telephone receiver, dialling the number she found on the pad.

'Hello?' Larry's tones cut across her turbulent thoughts.

'It's me—Sarah——'

'Sarah!' The surprise and pleasure in his voice came through strongly over the line. 'Tell me you're ringing to say I can take you up on that flight I promised you? You are, aren't you?'

'How did you guess?' she asked.

'Wishful thinking, I guess. I'll be over to collect you before you know it! The weather reporter on the radio keeps raving on about wind warnings later on in the day, so there's no time to waste. There are some super swimming beaches down the coast——'

'I'd like that!'

'Right, grab your bikini and your best sunhat—the sun's fierce at the beach, and with your English complexion——'

'I will,' Sarah assured him.

'Oh, one other thing. Up in the air it can get a bit cool. Three extra jumpers is the rule——'

She gasped. 'Did you say three? I don't think I need——'

'You'll feel a bit differently when you're eight hundred feet above the earth, believe me. Look, we'll make a day of it, have a picnic and a swim. You'll be in no danger at a surf beach, no matter how high the waves are. I'll take care of you.'

A faint warmth melted the block of ice that seemed to have set around her heart. Larry was kind and steady, and in spite of their short acquaintance she knew she could trust him. Not like Nick, who looked at her at times as if, in spite of their stormy arguments, he cared about her. And it all meant nothing—nothing, except maybe a few moments' dalliance with a girl who because of their working together he had got to know and like a little. While all the time he and Lynn—— How could she have been so gullible?

She brought her mind back to Larry's enthusiastic tones. 'I can't wait to get cracking! See you soon, and I mean *soon*!'

In the cottage she stuffed her bikini into a roomy cloth bag, threw in a towel, sunglasses, sun-block cream and a plastic eye-shade. Then she pulled extra T-shirts over her head and went to the house to find Kate.

The older woman was in the kitchen, where she was slicing up for jam a pile of misshapen kiwi-fruit that Penny had given her and which was not suitable for the export market. 'Larry's taking me for a flight in his microlight,' she told Kate. 'He'll be over to pick me up almost right away.'

Kate's blue eyes glinted with disapproval. 'Nick won't be pleased about that,' she observed grimly. 'I suppose you know he's away for the day with Lynn?'

But Sarah didn't want to hear about Lynn. A defiant flush stained her cheeks. 'No, he won't like it one little bit,' she agreed smoothly.

'What's going to happen——' Kate eyed Sarah challengingly '—if a tour party shows up and there's no one here to see to them?'

Sarah had an answer to that. 'I checked; there's no one booked in for today.'

'You never know when they'll arrive,' Kate said repressively, 'especially on a day like this. I hope you know what you're doing. I don't wonder Nick doesn't approve of your going up in that little plane, risking your life——'

Sarah threw her an incredulous look. 'With Larry's accident-free record——'

'That's just it! It must be about time——'

'Well, anyway, I'm going!' Sarah wasn't surprised that Kate didn't bid her goodbye.

She was waiting on the short grass when the machine floating on giant pink wings dropped down from a cloudless sky and raced over the grass. In a minute Larry had leaped down from the machine and was hurrying towards her, his face alight with excitement. 'It's great to see you again! I'd all but given up hope of taking you up for a flight, and now——' The warmth and feeling in his tone eased a little of the hurt and sense of betrayal that she couldn't seem to get out of her mind.

'Jump in!' He helped her to climb into one of the two small leather seats bolted to an aluminium frame. 'The motor might have a lawnmower-pull start, but it's got as much power as the largest engine. Say cheese!' He had whipped a camera from the pocket of his jeans.

Forcing a smile, Sarah struck a pose. 'Just to prove to myself that all this has really happened!'

He climbed into the pilot's seat. 'Right! We're away!' She heard his voice through the ear-muff as they shot over the grass.

Now that she was up in the sky she didn't feel at all scared. There was so much to see below—vast green paddocks dotted with grazing sheep, boundaries of macrocarpa trees running across steep hillsides. Soon they passed over high peaks covered with densely growing native bush and she found herself looking down on a patchwork of kiwi-fruit and citrus plantations, high mesh fences enclosing grazing deer. The next minute she caught her breath as she came in sight of the sea, dancing and sparkling with a myriad facets of sunlight. Far below the expanse of golden sand stretched away into the misty distance.

Presently Larry was guiding the machine down on a flat grassy area and soon they were making their way over sandhills studded with marram grass. Sarah could feel on her face the damp touch of blowing sea-spray and in her nostrils was the salty tang of the sea.

Presently they leaped down a bank to glistening wet sand below. 'Looking for a changing-shed?' Larry grinned. 'Stay right where you are!'

'Oh!' Sarah looked up at him enquiringly, then laughed. 'I see what you mean!' For above them towered a giant pohutukawa tree, its exposed roots snaking precariously down the sandy slope.

Swiftly she slipped into the shelter of the gnarled trunk, thankful to exchange the discomfort of her clothing for the cool freedom of her bikini. Placing her garments in a fork of the tree, she joined Larry, who was waiting for her on the sand, a gangling, sun-browned man clad in vividly patterned swim-shorts.

It was all unbelievably beautiful, she marvelled, looking around her. A sky so blue that you felt you could reach up and touch it, the diamond sparkle of the sea. Yet few people were here to enjoy the flawless stretch of the beach. Far out in the deep swimmers were riding their surfboards over the breakers, there were odd family parties grouped around a tent or Land Rover on the sand, but here there were only the gulls wheeling and crying over the waves. From nowhere came the thought, If only it were Nick who was here with me today. Sarah pushed the ridiculous notion aside. Nick was enjoying himself with Lynn, remember?

'Come on in!' Larry clasped her hand in his and together they ran over gleaming sand to plunge into the creaming foam at the water's edge and swim out beyond the breaking surf.

Suddenly Sarah realised that a great comber was surging towards her. The next moment the force of the wave caught her off balance and she felt herself plunging down, down into swirling green depths. As she floundered helplessly in the water Larry's strong hand wrenched her to the surface and breathlessly she dashed sea water from her eyes and pushed the streaming wet hair back from her forehead.

Under Larry's guidance it wasn't long before she mastered the skill of body-surfing. Again and again they made their way through the tossing waves to await an incoming breaker and be carried inshore.

It was a good way, she told herself between the onslaught of the waves, to free herself of thoughts of Nick, if only for a time.

At last they splashed through the shallows to throw themselves down on the warm sand and let the hot sun beat down on their bodies.

I'll remember this day when I'm back in England, Sarah thought. The remote beach, the clear, bright sunshine, the feeling of dreamy relaxation from the touch of sun and salt water drying on my skin. Once again a thought came unbidden. It would all be perfect if only Nick had been my companion. What was she thinking of?

'Penny for them?' Larry raised himself on an elbow to gaze down at her.

'Just nothing things.'

'That's OK, then. So long as you're not dreaming of some other guy.' He leaped to his feet. 'Stay right here—I won't be long!' He sprang up the bank, and she watched him crossing the sandhills, his long, tanned legs taking the shifting sands swiftly and effortlessly.

When he came back to her he was carrying a cardboard carton which he flung open with a flourish. 'Lunch, my lady?'

'I don't believe it!' Sarah selected a sandwich from the container. 'I didn't think you'd have time today to fix anything to eat.'

'I didn't!' He was handing her fruit juice from a coolbox. 'It was all rush-rush this morning, but Mum came to the rescue.'

'Your mum?' Somehow Sarah hadn't given any thought to Larry's family. It had not seemed of any importance to her. Only Nick mattered to her. Had mattered, she corrected herself, and *had* was the operative word. All at once the delicious food tasted like sawdust to her.

When the picnic meal was over they returned to plunge into the tossing surf and once again wade out into deep water to await the onslaught of the next wall of green that would carry them swiftly inshore. At last they wandered back to the beach to drop down on the sand, their faces upturned to the sun. She couldn't believe it when Larry, glancing down at the waterproof watch on his wrist, told her the time. How could so many hours have slipped by unnoticed?

Lulled by a delicious sense of relaxation, Sarah was dozing when she felt a touch on her lips and opened her eyes to find Larry bending over her, his warm breath on her face. The next moment he was raining kisses on her face, her neck, her throat. 'Sarah, darling.' His low tones were hoarse with passion.

'Don't!' In a swift movement she had jerked herself free of his embracing arms and sprung to her feet.

He stared up at her, eyes dark with surprise and anger. 'I thought you liked me?'

'I do like you! Of course I do! It's just——'

All at once his eyes were deep and intent. 'There's someone else, isn't there? Some guy over in England who's waiting to get you back with him, counting the days——'

She laughed the suggestion away. 'Not that I know of.'

'Someone here, then?' he persisted.

'How could there be?' Somehow she couldn't meet his searching gaze and looked away, a picture flashing on the screen of her mind. Nick, slim-hipped, sunbronzed. His smile that could do things to your emotions in spite of all your resolutions not to allow him to affect you that way.

He said very low, 'So long as I've got a chance.'

As they went over the shifting sand of the sandhills and climbed into the machine Larry switched back into her pleasant, undemanding companion. When they came in sight of the vineyard the sun was low in the sky. The next moment, trees, houses and vehicles went whizzing past as Larry grounded the plane at breakneck speed.

He helped her out of the machine, and, mindful of purple shadows misting the bush-clad hills around them, she bade him a swift farewell. 'It's been a fantastic day—I'll say goodbye—— '

'Wait!' Larry put out a hand to detain her. 'We'll do it again soon.' His light-hearted tone deepened to an anxious note. 'You'll ring me as soon as you can get a day free?'

Sarah said laughingly, 'I did, didn't I?'

His expression cleared. 'The best sound I ever heard, that telephone buzz this morning. Don't forget——'

'I won't! Bye.' She made to turn away, but he caught her close to him and bent over her, then his lips met hers in a passionate and lingering kiss. Abruptly he released her and, raising a hand in salute, climbed back into the plane.

She stood waving until the brilliant pink wings rose in the air to skim over the hills, then turned to find herself facing Nick's pale, strained features. His voice was low and unsteady. '*You're back*! You're so late, you had me worried stiff.' There was no mistaking his expression of unutterable relief. 'Hell.' He passed a hand over tousled hair. 'Don't ever do that to me again!'

Sarah stared at him in amazement. Why, he was speaking as if her safe return meant a lot to him, an awful lot. But of course, she reminded herself the next moment, he wouldn't want to lose his helper in the vineyard, especially one who happened to be intensely interested in wine production.

She wrenched her mind back to his relieved tones. 'I had to take off early today. A friend——' why must he tell her about Lynn? '—dropped in out of the blue. Seems she's been quietly married to a guy she met over in England on her last trip overseas. They've only known each other for a short time, but she tells me it's the real thing for both of them. Anyway, her husband has decided to give up his accountant's job in England for growing grapes out in New Zealand, having a shot at wine-making. He has some capital and he and Lynn have got wind of a property further south that might suit them, house and all. It was up for auction today, so there wasn't any time to spare. They put it to me to zip down and give the place the once-over, check that it has the right type of soil for grape growing, good climatic conditions, lying to the sun and all that. It was no problem—good investment and just the type of thing they were looking for. I told them to go right ahead, with my blessing.'

'Oh!' A sudden inexplicable happiness surged through Sarah.

'I shot off home as soon as I could,' Nick was saying, 'and then I heard about you.' A shadow crossed his face and she had to strain to catch the low words. 'It's been a long day. Then when it got so late... Do you realise that machine has only got one engine, and if it packs up——?'

'But it didn't!' She flashed him a confident smile. 'Tell me, did any tour parties arrive here while you were away?'

'A couple, so Kate told me.' He shrugged the matter away as of no consequence. 'They'll come back if they're interested.'

Could this really be Nick who was speaking? Sarah could scarcely believe her ears. She said in bewilderment, 'You don't mind my taking off for the day, then?'

'Mind?' His eyes seemed to soften and darken. 'I don't mind anything now that I've got you back with me!'

Her heart did a crazy somersault, then steadied. Idiot! she chided herself. With any other man the words might have conveyed a romantic significance. With Nick he was merely congratulating himself on not having lost his Girl Friday!

The thought sparked her to anger and her green eyes glittered. 'And I didn't know you cared!' she flung at him. The next moment she would have given anything to recall the words. He didn't even bother to reply to the taunt, but merely regarded her silently with an unreadable expression in his dark eyes. As always there was just no understanding him. Flushed with confusion, she muttered, 'I'd better get back to the cottage,' and hurried away.

As she went along the path her turbulent thoughts were still with Nick. Now she knew for sure that she had merely fancied any softening of his feelings towards her. Feeling deflated all at once, she went into the cottage, scarcely aware of her surroundings. If only... Suddenly the truth struck her with the force of a physical blow. She was deeply and irrevocably in love with a man who would never love her in return, who, was he to learn of her real position here, would utterly despise her. But he wouldn't find out, she vowed silently, not if she could help it!

Why hadn't she realised the truth before? Nick meant everything to her. He was her life. His nearness possessed her. And she had only a few weeks left before she must leave here for ever.

Little things hitherto unnoticed returned to mind to click into place. The golden days that had lost their lustre when Nick was absent from the vineyard on business. Her sudden rush of happiness when later she caught sight of his car turning in at the driveway. Seeing him, being with him, working alongside him, meant the world to her. And to Nick, her lips twisted despairingly, she was no more than an argumentative, difficult employee, albeit skilled at her work and a fast learner.

A wave of pain clutched Sarah's heart. If she had any pride or self-respect she would return to England by the first available plane. The trouble was, she thought bleakly, she didn't seem to possess either of those qualities. In the brief time remaining to her of her working holiday in the vineyard she couldn't bear to be parted from Nick for even a single day. Just being near him was all that mattered to her, fool that she was!

CHAPTER EIGHT

LYING in bed a little later, Sarah tossed and turned endlessly as the worrying thoughts crowded her mind. All the time a picture of Nick's laughing face rose before her mental vision. She loved him. Every little thing about him was precious to her. His crisply curling black hair, the heavily fringed dark eyes and his smile, his heart-stopping smile that made you forget everything else in the world, even her crazy masquerade that had seemed such a harmless deception at the time and had now taken on a desperate importance in her life.

If only there were some way in which she could continue to stay here, even if he never knew her feelings for him. Confess the whole story to him then, explain how she was here under false pretences and trust he would understand. *Some hope*! Nick, proud and independent, with his deep commitment to the vineyard he had worked up to make a name for itself in the world of wine. He would never forgive her for lying to him, pretending to be someone else. Worse, he might regard her as an impostor who had come here for the purpose of checking on his integrity, his honesty regarding the financial aspects of the vineyard.

What she should do, of course, would be to leave here at once and never see him again. At least that way she would be spared the pain of seeing the disillusionment in his eyes. A wave of misery flooded her. No, that she couldn't do.

Oh, she could send word to the lawyers in London directing that a higher salary be offered to Nick to stay on and manage Sunvalley on her behalf, but that wouldn't take away the ache of longing just to be with him, loving him, even if he never, ever cared for her in the way she cared for him.

She must have fallen asleep, for at some time during the night she was jolted awake by sounds of violent crashing and banging on the roof above her head. Burglars were up there, trying to make an entry into the cottage!

With fumbling fingers Sarah felt for the light-switch on the bedside table, knocking the lamp to the floor. As she scrambled from the bed she caught the sound of a dull thud somewhere in the house and the next moment she was aware of an unseen form brushing past her in the darkness. She wasn't even aware of the screams that echoed from her throat. 'Help me! Help me!' Still screaming in terror, she ran wildly through the dining-room and out of the back door. Then she was running over dew-wet grass towards the lighted house, straight into the arms of a masculine figure who was hurrying down the path towards her.

'Nick! It's you! It's you!' she gasped on a great breath of relief. A violent shudder racked her as she clung wildly to him.

'Hey!' He was clasping her trembling form. 'What's wrong?'

'Someone's inside the cottage!' she gasped. 'Burglars. They're wrecking the place! One of them rushed past me in the dark!' Shudders still racked her body, but another part of her mind was finding ineffable bliss in nestling close against Nick's shoulder.

'I'll check.' He didn't appear unduly concerned, she thought bewilderedly, but then hadn't he told her that there had been wine stolen from the bottle store in the past? The thought brought her panicky feelings back with a rush.

'No! Don't go in there!' she cried. 'They're crazy! They're vandalising the place—you should have heard the noise! They might have a gun——'

'I doubt it.' She caught the chuckle deep in his throat.

'What's so funny?' she whispered unsteadily.

'You'll see for yourself in a moment.'

She swallowed, then eyed him accusingly. 'You don't believe me, do you?'

'Sure I believe you! Relax, Sarah, there's nothing to be afraid of. Possums come out of the bush at night and climb up on the roof. They make a hell of a commotion up there, and now and again they crash down the chimney and scare the hell out of anyone who happens to be sleeping in the cottage. If they're trapped in a room they go completely haywire, knock down everything in sight in a mad panic to get outside. That's when the sharp claws come into play, but they won't hurt you otherwise; they're more scared of you than you are of them.'

'P-possums?' Sarah had never in her life felt so mortified. All that terrified screaming and carrying on——

'I'll show you.' Nick set her free. 'Coming?'

The bemusement of his nearness was still with her, and she swung confusedly aside, only to trip over her long, filmy nightdress that had somehow managed to get entangled around her bare feet. The next moment she found herself scooped up in his arms and he was striding towards the cottage. Soon they were moving through the porch and through the open door into the dining-room. Gently he set her down on the couch, then put a hand to the light-switch. 'Prepare for a surprise!'

The room sprang into life and she took a quick breath, her eyes dilated with shock as she took in the ravaged surroundings. China ornaments from the dresser lay shattered to fragments on the floor. A vase of flowers was overturned on the table, the water still trickling to the carpet, and everywhere there was black soot dislodged from the open fireplace.

'There goes your robber—or one of his mates!' Nick grinned wryly as a small furry animal dropped to the hearth in a fresh shower of soot to dash wildly past them and out through the open door into the night.

'Stay right there,' he said matter-of-factly, 'while I have a clean-up. Believe me, I'm an old hand at this game.'

Tucking her feet under the long nightdress, Sarah murmured, 'Thanks.' For once she had no wish to dispute his orders. There was a deep glowing look in his eyes that undermined all her defences, and, besides, there was something infinitely satisfying in watching him as, with deft fingers, he cleared away soot and dust, swept up broken china, mopped up water dripping from the table. Just as if, she mused dreamily, they were a man and a woman in love with each other and the cottage was their home. The next moment realisation of the true position between her and Nick came with a stab of the heart.

'Don't look like that.' His all-too-perceptive glance was taking in the wistful droop of her lips. 'All this will be as good as new in the morning.'

'I guess so.'

She made an effort to smile, but something in the clouded expression in her eyes must have got through to him, for he dropped down at her side. 'What's the problem?' Very gently he placed his hand beneath her chin, forcing her to meet his gaze. 'Something I've done? If it is——'

'No! No!' All the pent-up emotion she was feeling sent the betraying words flying unbidden to her lips. 'Not you, Nick! Never you!'

The next moment she was gathered in his arms, he was holding her close, and she went straight to heaven. Tenderly he ran his fingers down her cheek. 'I love you, Sarah.' She barely caught the huskily spoken words. 'I always have. I've wanted to do this for a long time——' His lips found hers in a kiss, tender at first, then deepening, and she gave herself up to the dangerous attraction against which she had struggled in vain since their first moment of meeting.

'I love you,' she whispered against his lips. Ardently she responded to his caress. A thousand candles seemed to have burst into flames around her and there was nothing in all the world but his nearness, his low, exultant tones. 'I'll always love you. You know that, don't you?'

'So much to plan for you and me, my darling, my love. For a start——' his words were punctuated with kisses '—you can cancel that return ticket to England right now. It's you and me from now on, Sarah; we belong together.'

It was a long time later when she roused herself from the shelter of Nick's arms. There were things that must be said. He loved her, she knew now, with a love that was deep enough to surmount any obstacle. Loving her, he would understand, realise that she hadn't intended to deceive him, that she hadn't thought it would matter, just an impulse, almost a fun thing at the time.

He seemed to zero in on her thoughts. 'No more mix-ups, getting our lines crossed,' he said softly. 'Just you and me together—for always.'

Once again he caught her close, and, swept along on a high tide of emotion, she put her arms round his neck to finger the dark curling hair, something she had so often longed to do.

'Just you and me,' she echoed dreamily. Then all at once she froze, a chill feathering its way down her spine. She drew herself free, and said hesitatingly, 'Nick, there's something... something I've got to tell you. It's—important——' Please God, she prayed, make him understand. Don't let me ruin everything now.

He dropped a light kiss on the tip of her nose. 'Nothing's all that important.' His voice was husky with emotion. 'Not right now.'

'But it is, it is...' Her voice died into silence as she searched her mind for words—the right words. At last she said very low, 'Something that happened in England.'

'Forget it!' He drew her close to him. 'You're trembling. There's nothing to be afraid of.'

But there was. 'You don't understand.' All at once she was clinging to him compulsively.

Gently he placed his fingers against her mouth, stopping the words that trembled on her lips. 'Tomorrow. We'll have all the time in the world then for all our plans for the future and everything else.' His low tones deepened, softened with emotion. 'Tonight is ours, my darling. Don't let's spoil it.'

His seeking lips found hers and she returned his caress with a passionate poignancy, powerless against the electric sweetness that was zigzagging its way through her, sweeping away everything else from her mind, carrying her far into an unknown territory—and undreamed-of ecstasy.

In the morning she slept late, to awaken filled with a delicious sensation of happiness and contentment. Nick loved her, just as she loved him. She hugged the knowledge to her. Now she could tell him all about her stupid deception, knowing that he would understand. Oh, he'd be extremely surprised, of course, but when she had explained to him how it had all come about he would be delighted to find that fate had taken a hand in making his dream of a man-and-woman team working together at Sunvalley come true. Caring, sharing, loving, making a go of things together.

She skipped breakfast. This morning she was too excited, too deliriously happy, to be hungry. All she wanted was to see Nick once again, catch the glow of adoration in his eyes when he caught sight of her.

She took a leisurely shower, then slipped on panties and bra, pulled over her head a lilac-coloured T-shirt hanging loose over white linen pedal-pushers. Then she thrust bare tanned feet into white canvas trainers and brushed her hair until it shone with the dark gleam of a tui's wing.

Out in the clear, bright sunshine she hurried along the path and went into the bottle store, but only Paul was there, his head bent low in concentration as he painstakingly attempted to fix a label to a bottle of the new wine.

'Morning!' Sarah was so bubbling over with happiness and excitement that she was finding it difficult to behave as though nothing had happened. 'Have you seen Nick this morning?' Even her voice betrayed her, she thought ruefully, but how could she help but reveal her elation when just saying Nick's name was a secret delight?

'Only for a minute.' Paul, intent on his task, gave no sign of having noticed her unusual state of mind. 'He said something about getting a phone call from some wine-growers from overseas. They've just arrived in the country and said they'd be calling in here some time today.'

'I'm glad you told me.' She dropped down to perch on an empty crate, smiling as she watched him. Right at this moment she would have smiled happily at anyone she happened to meet. She couldn't seem to concentrate on anything today for the wild sweet happiness that was singing along her nerves. At last she gathered herself together. 'Guess I'd better tune up my guitar strings.'

'I've got a guitar.' Paul raised an eager young face. 'Would you give me some lessons while I'm here?' His voice rang with enthusiasm. 'I could pay you the fees out of the wages Nick's paying me.'

She said laughingly. 'Why not?' Today she felt in a mood to offer help to anyone who requested it. She hadn't known she could feel such happiness. Aloud she said, 'You can use my guitar. The one I play doesn't really belong to me. And I don't want any payment!'

'Gee, thanks a lot, Sarah.' There was no doubting the warmth and sincerity of the boyish tones.

'It's nothing. Like me to give you a hand with that label? There's an easier way of doing the job. Look, I'll show you.' With deft fingers she fixed a label on a wine bottle, and Paul followed her example.

'I've got to go!' She had just at that moment through the open window caught sight of Nick working in the vineyard below. Her heart skipped a beat. After the most wonderful night of her life she couldn't wait to meet his warm gaze.

Slipping down from her perch, she hurried from the room and ran down the grassy rise leading to the vineyard. She was almost there when he came striding out from beneath a canopy of vines to meet her, his dark eyes glowing with warmth and love, just as she had known they would be. Lightly he threw an arm around her shoulders and bent to kiss her lips. 'You haven't forgotten last night?' he said tenderly.

'Last night?' A gleam of mischief lighted her eyes. 'You mean—the possums?'

His lambent glance held hers. 'Not altogether.' All at once his vibrant tones were alive with enthusiasm. 'We've got swags of plans for the future now that we'll be working here together. That is——' his lively dark eyes challenged her '—if you haven't changed your mind about the pattern of things here. You know? The traditional one of Sunvalley. A man and a woman, living right here on the premises, working side by side.'

Sarah looked up at him, all the love she had for him shining in her eyes. 'I haven't changed my mind.'

'That's all I wanted to know.' Taking her in his arms, he bent to kiss her lips.

When she could think straight once again she drew herself free. This was the moment to tell him about herself.

'Love you, Sarah!' Once again she was enfolded in his arms, and at his touch, the deep exultant happiness in his tones, her courage failed her and she couldn't bring herself to say the words.

This was Nick as she had never known him before. There was a sense of elation about him and the way in which he was looking at her... as if she was his whole world. All she had longed for had happened. She knew he was deeply in love with her, so why was she hesitating to say what must be said? The answer came unbidden. He was the type of man who would never let her down, while she—— All the misgivings she had refused to face crowded in on her, and her spirits dropped with a plop.

As they strolled together along the pathway it seemed to Sarah that her surroundings had never looked lovelier. Morning sunlight gilded the long spears of cabbage trees flicking their tufted heads in the warm soft breeze. Hibiscus blossoms flared scarlet, orange and coral in their full splendour and the sky was a blazing blue. All at once she was conscious of a heightened sense of perception. It was all a dream come true, Nick's love for her.

Then once again the dark shadow of apprehension sent her spirits plummeting. Would he feel the same way about her—after today?

'Don't look like that.' Raising her glance to his, she made an attempt at a light-hearted smile, but his searching glance hadn't missed the shadows in her eyes. Instantly he was all contrition. 'Tell me, if you're worried about staying on here we'll move out, start another vineyard somewhere else, anywhere you like.' They paused on the pathway and she couldn't avoid his questioning gaze.

'You're going to miss your aunt in England by staying out here?' he hazarded. 'Or she's going to miss you too much? Look, you can take a trip back there every year and catch up with her and the rest of your old friends. I've got it!' Once again his voice rang with enthusiasm. 'Your aunt can come to Sunvalley and live here with us. There's lots of room up at the house. If she wants to, that is. Whatever it is, sweet, that's on your mind, you've only got to let me in on it and I'll put it right!'

Oh, Nick, she breathed silently, would you? Would you *really*? Aloud she said hesitantly, 'It's something—— '

'Look, you can trust me,' he urged, 'whatever it is. Just try me. I——' His voice died away into a silence and she followed his gaze towards a late-model car that was turning in at the driveway. 'Hell,' he bit out disgustedly, 'we've got company! Some wine people from overseas I was expecting later in the day. Better go and meet them, I suppose,' he went on reluctantly. 'Come with me, Sarah.'

She hung back. 'But—you don't need me on the reception committee.'

He said quietly, 'I need you all the time for all my life. You *are* my life.'

How could she tell him the truth about herself—after that? But she would, later. An hour or so couldn't make any difference. Could it? Together they moved up the grassy rise, and Nick stepped forward to greet the group of wine-makers who stood by the office door awaiting his arrival. At the last moment another man climbed from the car and came to join the rest of the group. A tall, thin masculine figure wearing a green sports shirt and cream-coloured trousers. The stranger seemed to Sarah to be oddly familiar, and she searched her mind. Where before had she seen the thin frame, the pleasantly ugly face and tired eyes beneath horn-rimmed glasses? She couldn't pinpoint where she had met him. The next moment recognition came with sickening certainty. Of course—the New Zealand journalist with whom she had sat on the long flight from England. Every muscle in her body tensed with shock and dread. Had she confided to him the fairy-tale account of her coming to stay in the New Zealand vineyard? At the time she had been over the moon with excitement. She might well have told him the whole story. If only she could remember! she thought distractedly.

With some other part of her mind she realised that Nick was making introductions, turning towards her. 'Sarah, this is——'

'Hi, Sarah! Great to see you again!' The journalist took her hand in his firm clasp. 'Remember me? Ewan? We met on the plane trip from England a few weeks ago. I told you I'd be looking you up to see how you're making out with the new venture.' He swung around to turn a laughing face to Nick. 'Believe me, it's not on every plane trip you come across a girl who's been lucky enough to inherit a vineyard on the other side of the world! Not just a vineyard either, but one with an international reputation for top-quality wines!'

Sarah froze. In the stunned silence her gaze went to Nick, and she knew that her own expression of shock and horror had left him in no doubt as to the truth of Ewan's words. All too clearly Nick had taken a shattering blow, his features set and implacable as a man's face carved in stone.

Ewan's puzzled glance moved from Nick to herself and he gave an uneasy laugh. 'Joke,' he said weakly.

'It's OK.' Nick shrugged the subject away.

Dazedly Sarah realised that he was continuing to make the introductions. His words seemed to be coming from a distance. 'Sarah *Smith*.' His sardonic emphasis on the name cut her to the heart. 'Sarah's a seasonal worker here, one of my assistants.' Somehow she managed to produce some sort of smile, nodding pleasantly to the visitors. But all the time the hurtful thoughts were chasing through her distraught mind. 'Sarah Smith,' he had said, not 'Sarah Sinclair', the name by which he knew her. 'One of his seasonal workers.' Clearly this was Nick's way of putting her right back into the place where she belonged, a girl who was no more to him than a casual worker in the vineyard.

As he continued to speak with the tour party it seemed to her that his manner appeared much as usual. It was his eyes, she thought in desolation, that were different—cold, hard, formidable. And his voice—Nick's pleasant tones with all the laughter fled from them. As he guided the group from the room he didn't again glance towards Sarah's stricken face.

She stared after him, trembling. What had she expected? she asked herself bitterly. It was over, all those shining hopes and dreams. Nick would need to love her an awful lot to forgive this deception. Love? He would be glad to be rid of her, she thought bleakly.

All at once she became aware that Ewan had not left the room with the rest of the group. As he came towards her she thought illogically that the lines scored down either side of his thin face seemed to have deepened.

'Sorry, Sarah,' he said, very low. 'I guess I made a blue that time! I should have caught on that night on the plane trip that you were stringing me a line to pass away the time. Fantasy stuff, of course. But you sure took me in. I could have sworn that tale you spun me was for real. Too good to be true in real life, of course— I should have known!' His eyes were shadowed with regret. 'What can I say?'

She murmured half under her breath, 'It wasn't your fault.'

'All the same...' Through the open doorway his glance went to Nick as the latter escorted the tour party in the direction of the cellars.

'It doesn't matter.' Her voice was utterly without hope. 'Nothing matters now,' she whispered, overcome by anguish too deep for words.

Suddenly his voice sharpened. 'It's not true, that story you gave me on the plane coming over? It *is*, isn't it? You're not telling me,' he said incredulously, 'that you haven't told him who you really are? That the guy who runs the place here doesn't know you're the owner?'

Sarah said tonelessly, 'It's true, and he doesn't't——' her voice wobbled '*—didn't* know until now. I was going to let him in on how things were today.' She heard her own desolate tones as though listening to another girl speaking. 'I didn't mean it to be this way when I came here——' She broke off, recalling her high spirits on the plane trip from England, her wild happiness born of the incredibly wonderful events that had transformed her ordinary everyday life.

'Go on.' Ewan's eyes were deep and intent.

She drew a deep breath. Confession time. She might as well get used to it. She had a lot of explaining to do, and Nick—— Don't think about Nick! she told herself.

'When I arrived here Nick's aunt didn't want to have anything to do with me. She's the housekeeper at the vineyard and she thought——' Her voice faltered.

He nodded, his eyes sombre. 'I can imagine. Resented you being the new owner. Thought Nick should have inherited the vineyard. It's only natural.'

Her deadpan tones flowed on. 'Something like that. Anyway, just when Kate had about thrown me out on the road Nick arrived to join us. He was expecting an answer to an ad he'd put in the local paper wanting a girl to help out in the vineyard for a few weeks, and he thought I—I——'

'I get it. So you grabbed the chance to stay on at Sunvalley and have a look around the property that way?'

She nodded. 'It was so easy. You see, I happened to have changed my name, except the Sarah, years ago, and even mail from relatives in England would be addressed to me here by the name I called myself—Sarah Sinclair. All I had to do was to rip off the Air New Zealand label from my travel bag. I had to use my real name on my passport and travel documents. I didn't think it would hurt anyone.' Her low tones died away into silence.

'Nick's sure hurting now. I saw his face when I blew the whole thing. I could kick myself,' Ewan added morosely.

She said slowly, despairingly, 'He had to know some time. I was planning to tell him today. Now it's too late.'

The hopeless finality of her tone must have got through to him, for suddenly his expression changed to one of surprise and dismay. 'You're not saying you and Nick are——?'

She nodded and said raggedly, 'We were.'

For a moment he regarded her silently, his eyes dark with compassion and regret. 'Tough. Look, if I can do anything, anything at all to put things right——'

She shook her head. 'You can't. No one can.' She made an attempt to force her voice to a careless note. 'Just one of those things, I guess, not the end of the world.'

He shot her a perceptive glance. 'I'd believe you if you didn't look as though you've taken one hell of a knock.'

'My own fault. It seemed such a good idea—at the time.'

He frowned. 'And I had to blow it.'

'You weren't to know,' came her heavy tones. 'Anyway, I'll be going back to England in a day or so.'

'I'm real sorry.' Ewan's warm handclasp underlined the expression of concern in his craggy features. He hesitated. 'Sure you'll be all right?'

She nodded. 'Don't worry about me. I've just got to pull myself together and get on with living.' The brave words were spoiled by the quiver in her voice. 'Anyway——' she drew a deep breath '—right now I'm supposed to be in the reception-room to play my guitar and entertain your group at lunch.'

His gaze was on her trembling hands. 'Reckon you can make it?'

Sarah gave a shaky smile. 'I've just got to.' Moving like a girl in a trance, she crossed the room to open a cupboard and take out a guitar.

Together they moved along the path to the reception-room, where Sarah went to stand in the shadows in a corner of the lounge. She sent Ewan a wobbly smile. 'Wish me luck!'

At Nick, arriving the next moment with the tour party, she didn't look. That was something she couldn't face, not yet. Instead she bent low over the instrument, fingering the strings. Presently the buzz of masculine voices died away as her pure young tones echoed around the room and out through open windows into the pine-scented air. Familiarity with the melodies she was singing came to her aid, and almost without volition she managed to get through the ordeal successfully.

Afterwards she found herself seated at her desk in the office without any realisation of how she had got there. Dazedly she tried to bury herself in an account book, her gaze fixed on the long columns of figures that made no impression on her mind. In an abandonment of grief she told herself over and over again, If only I could have told him myself. I could have explained how it wasn't planned, the way I'd deceived him, and maybe, just maybe he would have believed me. But now...

The long hours dragged on. At some time in the afternoon she jerked herself to awareness to find Ewan moving towards her desk. The next minute he was standing beside her, and she raised heavy eyes to his concerned face.

'I'm off now. The others are waiting in the car. Just wanted to make sure you're all right.'

She tried to smile, but she didn't make a very good job of it. 'I'm fine, truly.'

'You don't look it.' His searching gaze took in her pale cheeks and apathetic expression. 'Sorry about all this,' he murmured diffidently. 'There doesn't seem anything else I can say except goodbye. Maybe I'll see you again some other time.'

She shook her head, forcing back the tears that threatened to spill over, knowing that for her there would be no other time. She would never be at Sunvalley again, and it was all her own fault!

When Ewan had left her she stared unseeingly from the window at the cars and trucks clustered in the driveway. Nick was standing near a mini-van, welcoming new arrivals, and all at once she realised that he was guiding the tour party towards the bottle store. With an effort she gathered her senses together, and, hurrying from the office, she was ready and waiting when a few minutes later Nick appeared with the group.

She glanced up to meet his cool, hard stare. 'This is Sarah,' he told the party who had gathered around him. 'If you want to try out any of the wines just ask her. She'll be happy to help you. She works here.'

'Of course.' She forced a smile through stiff lips, her heavy-eyed glance taking in the strangers. But all the time other thoughts were rushing through her distraught mind. There had been a cutting edge to Nick's tones. Once again he was placing her firmly back where she belonged in his scheme of things at Sunvalley. No one special. Just a girl who worked at the vineyard. *A girl who had tricked and betrayed him*. The closed expression in his dark eyes said it all.

The interminable day came to an end at last, and Sarah closed the door of the office and hurried along the path towards the cottage—and sanctuary. Dropping down to the couch in the living-room, she surrendered to an abandonment of grief, letting the tears she had forced back for so many hours trickle unchecked down her cheeks.

Later, when shadows were falling across the uncurtained windows, a peremptory knocking penetrated Sarah's numbed mind. Hastily brushing away the tears from her eyes with the back of her hand, she went to answer the summons. Only one person she knew would beat a thunderous tattoo on the door like this.

The next moment she found herself facing Nick, his lean, dark figure silhouetted against the light of sunset. Even in the fading light she could see that his face was pale with anger.

She forced her voice to a steady note. 'Come in.'

He ignored the invitation, standing motionless, one hand hooked in the low-slung leather belt of his denim jeans. 'You *are* Sarah Smith,' his savage tone flayed her, 'the girl who's inherited the property here? Oh, don't bother to deny it; you look as guilty as hell!'

'Yes, I am, but it's not the way you think!' The words tumbled wildly from her lips. 'I would have told you, truly! I nearly did this morning, only——'

'Only——' his lips twisted sarcastically '—you didn't have the guts——'

'If you'd just let me explain,' she burst out desperately.

'More lies?' He brushed away her words with an impatient gesture of his hand. 'Why not admit that you planned the whole thing before you ever came here? Congratulations!' She winced at his insulting tone. 'You very nearly got away with it! You would have if your travelling mate hadn't come here and blown your story out of the window! If I hadn't been such a blind fool,' he ground out, 'I wouldn't have been so easily taken in.'

Sarah felt sick in her midriff. He might just as well have said, 'If I hadn't fallen in love with you——'

She said very low, 'I would have told you last night, but——'

'Forget last night!' His harsh tone flayed her.

'*Please* listen,' she begged, her youthful face pleading.

'Why should I——' she steeled herself to ignore the barb in his voice '—when I know exactly what you're going to say? Was it you or your lawyer who came up with the bright idea of checking up on me? This guy who's in charge of the show—why not take a trip out to the vineyard and check up on him? New Zealand's a heck of a long way away from here. He could have been getting away with murder! After all, he worked on the vineyard for years and he's been in sole charge of the place since the owner died. It would be easy for him to fake the books, get away with thousands of dollars. He could swing it easily if he wanted to put his mind to it. And the way the sales figures for Sunvalley wine have been mounting... might even consider he was entitled to a share of the profits, a bit more than a manager's salary, in the circumstances. He's the obvious choice to keep on as manager of the estate. All the more reason to make sure he's honest and reliable. No need for you to let on who you are—you'll never find out anything important that way. Better to turn up there as an English girl looking for holiday work during the summer. It will be time for harvesting the grapes in that part of the world, so why not give it a go? And don't tell me it wasn't like that!' He shot the words at her like bullets.

The cruel accusations tore her apart. 'No!' she cried. 'You're wrong——'

'Am I?' His cutting tone ripped across her quivering nerves. 'Oh, sure you were rapt in finding out all you could about wine-making, selling, the lot. You wanted to learn the trade, you told me. True enough,' he said with bitter irony, 'even if it was for reasons of your own——'

Trembling, Sarah cut in, 'I was interested!'

'I'll bet. Tell me, are you quite satisfied with your undercover investigations? No complaints about the manager—sorry, *temporary* manager? Oh, don't worry, I'll stay on here until such time as you can make arrangements for someone else to take over. Shouldn't be too difficult, with a thriving vineyard like Sunvalley.'

She said very low, 'No one could run the vineyard the way you do. You *are* Sunvalley.'

'Glad you appreciate my efforts.' Nick's cold, satirical tones cut deep.

All at once frustration and heartache gave place to a rush of hot anger. It was hopeless trying to convince him of the truth; the odds were stacked against her. Her green eyes glinted. But whether he believed her or not he was going to listen to her. She faced him spiritedly. 'You've got it all wrong! I didn't dream of coming out here as an—an ordinary girl. When I got word about the inheritance in New Zealand I was so excited, I just couldn't wait to come out here to stay and get to know something of the working life of the vineyard. Steven had told me so much about it, I felt I knew a lot about it already. I told the lawyers in London not to let you know I was coming. I thought it would be fun to make it a surprise visit——'

'Fun?' he said bitterly. 'Is that what you call it?'

Sarah steeled herself to ignore the bitterness of his tone. 'Then when I arrived here Kate took one look at the Air New Zealand label on my travel bag and was sure I was the girl who'd inherited Sunvalley. "That awful girl from England'', she called me. She just about ordered me off the property, and I knew I'd never be able to stay here, not even for a single night. And then,' her words came in a rush, 'you came along and mistook me for a girl from overseas looking for holiday work in the vineyard. And you wanted me——' She stopped short, cursing herself for her unfortunate choice of words. The next moment she made the blunder worse by correcting herself. 'When you said I could work here I just——' she drew a deep breath '—grabbed the opportunity. There didn't seem to me to be any harm in such a simple deception at the time. I planned to go back to England at the end of summer and I didn't think we'd ever meet again. So what did it matter?'

Nick made no comment, and his silence was somehow more daunting than his cold, angry stare. What was he thinking? The answer came unbidden. He despises me, that's what!

She wrenched her mind back to his mocking drawl. 'Just too bad that your journalist friend gave the game away! To give him his due, he did his best to cover for you. I'm not blaming him——'

'No, but you're blaming *me*!' Two crimson spots of colour burned high in her cheeks and her eyes were shooting sparks. 'No matter what I tell you, you won't believe me, will you?'

'Why should I?' His lazy drawl was maddening.

It was clear that no matter how hard she tried to explain matters to him he refused to listen to her. Her soft lips firmed determinedly. She was determined to go down with all flags flying. 'Anyone would think,' she burst out, 'that I'd deliberately planned the whole thing.'

'Didn't you?'

'No!' she flung at him. 'I keep telling you! Anyway...' All at once the dark cloud of anger that had mushroomed up inside her died away. 'I want you to have the vineyard and the money and everything that was left to me by Steven. It's yours really,' she went on in a voice choked with emotion. 'I've felt badly about the inheritance ever since I realised how things were here. Just a mistake.' Her voice thickened. 'I'll arrange with the lawyers in London to draw up a transfer as soon as I get back.'

'Oh, yes?' His brilliant gaze mocked her. 'Don't give me that! It won't wash, not after all the other lies you've handed out to me.'

'All right, then!' she flared. 'You don't need to put up with me much longer! I'm leaving just as soon as I can alter the booking on the plane. I'll ring through to the agents in town today and with any luck——' she faced him defiantly '—I'll be on my way to the airport tomorrow.'

'You won't, you know,' came his lazy drawl.

Fighting back tears, Sarah stared back at him, her small chin lifted challengingly. 'You can't stop me.'

'Can't I? I happen to need you, Sarah.'

'Need me?' Her heart did a crazy somersault, then she jerked her senses back to sanity. How fatally easy it was to slip back into yesterday's golden dreams.

'In the office,' he went on smoothly. 'Actually you owe me two weeks' notice of leaving my employ. A verbal agreement, if you remember?'

'I don't...' Her voice died away bewilderedly. Her mind was in such a turmoil that she couldn't clearly recall the details of their conversation at the time she had agreed to take the job in the vineyard. She became aware of his mocking tones.

'But of course you wouldn't honour a verbal agreement. Just a matter of integrity, really, something you wouldn't know about.'

Outraged, she spluttered angrily, 'Of course I'll stay for two weeks while you find someone else to take my place.'

Nick shrugged broad shoulders. 'So long as I know,' he murmured carelessly. 'So that about wraps everything up.'

All at once the finality of his words overwhelmed her. It was over, everything she had thought to be within her grasp. It couldn't end like this. But it had, right at this moment. Aloud she said raggedly, 'I suppose so,' and fled inside the cottage before the tears came.

CHAPTER NINE

IN THE morning Sarah made an effort to pull herself together. There were matters that must be attended to, and somehow she had to play her part and get through the days. But how could she get through the next fourteen days, feeling the way she did, loving Nick, leaving him for ever? She forced her heavy thoughts back to the present. First of all she must see Kate. Somehow she felt that Nick would not have divulged her real position at the vineyard to anyone else. Her soft lips curved wryly. No doubt he had his own reasons for keeping silent on the matter.

She found Kate in the sunny kitchen, busy spooning muffin mixture from a basin into tins on the bench. 'Morning, Kate!' Taking a deep breath, she went on in a rush of words, 'I just wanted to let you know that I'll be leaving here in a couple of weeks...' Becoming aware of Kate's shrewd glance taking in her red and swollen eyelids, Sarah trailed into silence.

'*Leaving*?' Kate looked so astonished that Sarah forced her voice to a careless tone.

'That's right. The job was only a temporary one, of course, and I've been here for quite a while.' She added lamely, 'And now that something's come up at—at—home——'

Kate, however, didn't appear to be listening. In a softened tone of voice Sarah had never heard her use before she said, 'Does Nick know about this?'

Did the other woman suspect the truth? Sarah wondered uneasily. Aloud she said quietly, 'He knows.'

'Hey! What's that you're saying?' Paul had come into the room, his eyes filled with dismay. 'You're not leaving Sunvalley!' he wailed. 'You can't! How about my guitar lessons?'

'Sorry about that.' Sarah was scarcely aware of what she was saying. 'But I've got to get back to England sooner than I thought.' At his downcast expression she felt a stab of compunction. 'Tell you what! If you like I'll give you a crash course, a lesson each night after work until I leave. How's that? It will get you started with the guitar—just the basics, of course—and after that it will be up to you to keep practising what you've learned until you can find another teacher to help you along.' To herself she was saying, Why not help him with guitar lessons? It will be something for me to do in the evenings in the time that's left, stop me thinking all the time of Nick, regretting... She wrenched her mind back to the boyish tones.

'I guess it'll have to do,' he murmured reluctantly.

Seated at the typewriter a short while later, Sarah stared unseeingly at the machine, the painful thoughts revolving endlessly in her mind. How could she endure the torture of being near Nick, seeing him daily, hearing him speak, *loving him*? All the time she was steeling herself to endure the anguish of meeting his formidable hard stare on the unavoidable occasions when he found it necessary to speak to her.

As the days went by it seemed to her that Nick spent a lot of his time away from the vineyard. Her imagination? Or could he be deliberately avoiding any contact with her? Not because he loathed her but because he too was sick at heart? But of course, she chided herself the next moment, that was mere wishful thinking on her part. The only feelings he had for her were bitterness and contempt. Hadn't he spelled it out quite clearly that all he wanted now was to cut her out of his life for ever?

Then all at once time was slipping by with frightening rapidity. Her last two days at Sunvalley! Already her freshly laundered T-shirts and shorts were folded and packed away in her travel bag. Not that she had accumulated many possessions during her stay, she mused ruefully. The shopping spree in the city that she had planned had not eventuated, and except for one magic day when together she and Nick had chosen the dress for her to wear at the wine festival she had not been far from the vineyard. Even though she hadn't realised it at the time she had been too happy here with Nick to want to leave Sunvalley even for a day. A lump like a chip of ice rose in her throat. She still felt that way. Determinedly she threw the travel bag aside and went into the bathroom to wash her hair. Anything to keep herself busy, to stop the thinking, the longing. Soon she was holding a blow-drier over the dark strands.

'No need for you to worry about work the last couple of days,' Nick had told her in the flat, impersonal tones that chilled her afresh each time she heard them. 'I'll run you to the airport to get the plane. We'll hit the road first thing in the morning.'

Sick with misery, she could only nod and say, 'Thanks.'

'I'll check with the airport beforehand to make sure the flight will take off on time,' he had added. 'You never know what can happen.'

'Yes, of course.' But she meant 'yes' to his last few words, and crossed her fingers in a wish for the plane to be delayed. Would you mind, Nick, would you really mind if I weren't leaving here for ever? For a horrifying moment she imagined she might have spoken the words aloud, but evidently he had no inkling of her feelings towards him. Or if he had he made a good job of suppressing his suspicions.

Down in the valley the vines were already turning to a pale golden shade and the summer, her special summer, was waning. Now there remained only one matter that must be attended to, and that was to drop in on Penny and Bill and make her farewells. In a slack period of the kiwi-fruit production they had taken advantage of the quiet period to visit Penny's parents in another part of the country, but now they were home. She could see the front door wide open, sunshine streaming into the comfortably furnished lounge. A little later she had almost reached the gate when Penny waved a friendly hand from the porch and came to meet her.

'Hi!' Sarah dropped a kiss on Penny's suntanned cheek. 'Lovely to see you again. I thought you were never coming back!' She did her best to produce a genuine smile, unaware of the dark shadows around her eyes.

'Come on inside.' Penny led the way through the porch. 'I've got lots to tell you.'

Sarah dropped down to a cane chair. 'Are you feeling well? You look well. Baby behaving itself?'

'Oh, yes, I'm feeling just fine, and he's sure making his presence felt!'

Sarah roused herself from her heavy thoughts to say teasingly, 'He?'

'That's right. Bill's sure it's going to be a boy, and if it is he'll be named Nick.' Penny's plump cheeks dimpled. 'We both agree on that!'

'What if it's a girl?'

'Would you believe—Sarah?'

Sarah felt a pang of the heart. If only... Aloud she said, 'You two must be short on imagination if those are the only names you can dream up.'

'Why not?' Penny smiled. 'The two nicest people we know. You and Nick. You two are special.'

To change the subject Sarah said quickly, 'I'll make the coffee today. You sit down and take it easy for a change.'

'I think I'll take you up on that.' Penny eased herself down to a chair. 'It's just the heat.' She fanned her flushed face with a handkerchief.

In the blue and white painted kitchen Sarah went to the Dutch dresser, and found pottery mugs and instant coffee. When they were settled once again in the lounge, steaming coffee-mugs set on the glass-topped table between them, Sarah leaned forward and forced her voice to an interested inflexion. 'Now tell me all about your holiday,' she urged warmly. 'Where did you go? What did you do? Did you see any shows in the city?'

'Did we ever!' Penny launched into a vivid description of the holiday. 'We enjoyed every minute of it——' All at once she paused. 'You're not listening,' she accused laughingly.

'I am!' Sarah tried to make her voice animated. 'Really I am!'

'You're not, you know. I can tell. Something on your mind?'

Sarah hesitated, nervously twisting a strand of dark hair round and around her finger. 'That's what I came to tell you,' she said slowly. 'I'm leaving here the day after tomorrow. I have to go back to England——' she avoided Penny's eyes '—sooner than I expected.' She tried to hide her trembling hands but, meeting the other girl's compassionate gaze, she knew that it was too late for subterfuge.

'We'll miss you,' said Penny.

Sarah raised heavy eyes. 'Me too.'

'You won't be coming back, then?'

Sarah shook her head. The memories would be too painful, and to face Nick each day after what had happened, after that brief glimpse of all that life together could have meant... Aloud she murmured, 'Nick's taking me in to the airport to catch the plane on Thursday morning.'

'I know.'

'What?' Sarah's eyes widened in surprise. 'But how could you?'

'Nick was waiting here when we got home late last night. I guess he was in such a state of nerves that he just had to confide in someone. He let us into all that's been happening between you two while we've been away. After the things he said to you he's just about frantic with remorse and misery. He worships the ground you tread on, and he can't face your leaving him for ever.'

For a moment a wild hope lighted Sarah's eyes, then almost at once it died away. She said very low, 'He despises me.' She added slowly, 'Then he told you about me——?'

'Oh, yes, he let us into the Sarah Smith story and all that——'

'I didn't dream of pretending to be a student from overseas looking for seasonal work here,' Sarah broke in, 'until I got to the house and Kate showed me the door. Now I know he'll never forgive me for deceiving him. He made that quite clear.'

'That's not the way he's thinking now,' said Penny.

It took a moment or so for the incredible words to sink in. 'You're not telling me,' Sarah said on a breath, 'that he believes all I told him about the whole idea of what I did being just a fun thing at the time? You don't mean——?'

Penny nodded. 'He believes your story now. He's more than sorry that he blew his top at the time he found out who you really were. Says he should never have doubted you, "knowing the sort of girl you are".'

Sarah sighed. 'I'd like to believe it, but ever since he's known the truth about me he's been so—changed. He never looks directly at me if he can help it, and if he does his eyes are different—cold and hard. As if he hated me.'

'He's crazy about you—anyone can see it.'

'He doesn't look at me that way——'

'That's because he doesn't want you to guess at his real feelings. It doesn't mean he's stopped loving you.'

'But—but——' A happiness Sarah had thought gone for ever seemed almost within her grasp. And yet——

'Why doesn't he tell me all this himself?' She braced herself. 'I expect he will—soon,' she murmured uncertainly.

'He'll never tell you.' Penny's voice was soft with compassion. 'You may as well have it straight. For one thing, he's convinced you'd never believe he's changed his mind about the truth of your story, but it's more than that. As I said, he's so darned proud, nothing would induce him to ask you to stay on here with him. Not now.'

'You mean,' Sarah said slowly, 'because of my inheriting the vineyard and all that? But it makes no difference——'

'Nonsense! It makes all the difference in the world. Not to you, maybe, but to him everything is changed. Can you imagine the position he finds himself in now, with you the owner of the vineyard while he's just the manager—*if* you decide to keep him on in charge of the place? He's sure that, even if he could get you to believe he's changed his mind about all you told him being the truth, he can never ask you to stay on here——'

'We were going to be married,' Sarah broke in, 'to live here, work here together. He was over the moon with happiness, and then I spoiled it all.'

'He had to know some time,' said Penny. 'Nothing Bill and I could say would convince him that to ask you to stay on here as his wife would not be utterly useless. That you wouldn't think, after all that's happened, the property being willed to you and all that, that he'd be marrying you to get the vineyard back for himself. Bill and I argued with him for ages. We begged him to at least give you a chance to make your own decision, but we got nowhere. "A cheap fortune-hunter with an eye to the main chance, taking a mean advantage to get Sunvalley back for himself." That's the way you'd think of him, he told us, and nothing we could say to the contrary could shake him.'

'But I'd never feel that way about Nick!' Sarah cried in distress. 'I'd give the world to have things back as they were between us, only with no more secrets.' She raised an impassioned face to Penny's sympathetic gaze. 'I love him...so much.' Suddenly alarm rang in her voice. 'There must be something I could do,' she cried desperately, 'some way of persuading him how I feel about all this. If only he'd let me speak to him.'

Penny's eyes were thoughtful. 'That darned pride of his! And once Nick gets an idea into his head——'

'I know, I know. And I've only one clear day left.'

'And a night.' There was an odd, enigmatic note in Penny's voice. 'Oh, you'll think of something.' All at once her tone lightened. 'I almost forgot to tell you. We've asked a few friends in tomorrow night just to say goodbye. Nothing formal, just the locals, folks who know you. You'll be free to come?'

'I only wish I weren't,' Sarah said on a sigh. In her mind she was going over and over all that Penny had told her. Now that everything was changed and she knew Nick loved her——

Penny's voice broke across her musing. 'Bring your guitar with you, will you? Someone's sure to want you to give a number.'

Sarah turned a blank face towards her. 'If you want me to,' she murmured tonelessly, only half aware of her friend's request.

Sarah approached her last night at Sunvalley with a heavy heart. Despite all her thinking and planning, the endless night she had spent tossing and turning, at last she was forced to resign herself to the fact that she was leaving here in the morning and there was just nothing she could do about it. If only she had been able to speak to Nick, maybe she could have convinced him of her own thoughts in the matter of cutting all ties between them. But almost as if he divined her intention he had been absent from the house all through the day, and Kate had mentioned that he wouldn't be back until it was time for him to attend the social evening that Penny and Bill had planned as a farewell to Sarah.

Now there was only just time for her to get ready for the gathering, and somehow she had to nerve herself to get through the evening ahead. Her glittery black dress still hung in the wardrobe, but she wouldn't wear it ever again. It held too poignant a memory of the day she and Nick had chosen it together for her to wear at the wine festival.

Instead she put on a white muslin blouse, tying around her slim waist a swirling floral cotton skirt that was all she could produce in the way of a gala garment.

An impulse she couldn't define made her reach up to open a cupboard at the top of the wardrobe, one place she had neglected to check when she had packed her belongings for the journey back to England. Just as well to make sure. Standing on tiptoe, she ran an exploratory hand over the dark shelf. Nothing there—but wait! There was something that felt like a bundle of cloth and a folded sheet of paper of some sort, probably a forgotten magazine. The next moment she found herself gazing down in surprise at a crumpled ball of gossamer-fine material in shadings of rose and salmon-pink. Of course—the traditional Yugoslav dress about which she and Nick had argued so hotly. And not only the dress. Smoothing out the paper, she realised that she was holding a faded sheet of printed music. She recalled her anger, remembered hurling the music and the dress, crumpled into a ball, high in a corner of the dark cupboard, out of sight. She had wished never to set eyes on either of the articles again.

Her eyes misted with unshed tears. How trivial it all seemed now—that stormy encounter when neither she nor Nick would give in to the other's wishes.

Out of the past something niggled at the back of her mind. Something important. What were those challenging words she had flung at Nick in the heat of anger? A tape rolled back and the taunting implication of her words came back to mind with an odd intensity: The day I wear your traditional costume and play and sing the music you want me to will be the day I'm telling you I want to stay on here forever—with you!

A fit of trembling seized her. She had found a way to change everything that had gone wrong between her and Nick. Or had she? Anyway, it was worth a try. And what had she got to lose?

Swiftly she shook out the folds of the dress. It wasn't even crushed, so fine was the material. And she had the words and music of the song right here in her hand. Her heart was beating fast. Suppose I wear the dress tonight, this last night, sing the song—will he remember? And if he does... She knew now that he would never ask her to stay on here with him, so it was up to her to ask him. It was as simple as that. She had only one opportunity to carry out her sneaky plan. Risky, quite absurd really—and yet, and yet... It was her chance of happiness, and all at once she was determined to take full advantage of it.

Dropping down to the bed, she picked up the guitar, plucking the strings as she went over the melody. It was odd, but both words and music of the gum-digger's ballad seemed imprinted on her mind. At the rousing beat of the chorus her senses quickened. Defeat and frustration fell away and suddenly she was confident, excited. Her spirits rose on a great wave of hope.

All at once she caught a glimpse of her face in the mirror, no longer drawn, pale, defeatist, but bright-eyed—a girl with a purpose. If only it worked. It *must* work. To prove her faith in herself she unzipped her travel bag and slid out the name on the airport label. Please, God, she prayed silently, make the miracle happen. Make me not board that London plane tomorrow.

The sense of elation was still with her that evening when she arrived at the house to find Kate awaiting her on the lighted porch—a Kate she scarcely recognised, with frizzy hair subdued into neat waves and wearing a cool floral silk dress of dark blue shadings that complemented the colour of her eyes.

Sarah forced a smile. 'I see you're all ready.'

'Oh, yes, I wouldn't want to be late tonight. You know, Sarah...' Kate's tone was warm and regretful '...I'm going to miss you when you've gone.' The knowledge that Kate, brusque of speech and chary of compliments, had grown to like her was cheering, until Sarah realised that of course Nick would not have told her who she, Sarah, really was. The brief moment of happiness died away.

'Nick's gone on ahead,' Kate was saying as she and Sarah went down the steps and out into the soft night air. 'I don't know what's got into him lately,' she complained as they took the path leading to the gate. 'He's not usually moody, but the last few days—I suppose it's got something to do with business. He's been in a bad mood ever since that last visit of wine-growers from overseas two weeks ago.'

'You can say that again!' Paul hurried through the darkness to join them. 'Boy, am I glad to get away from Nick!' he told Sarah. 'I can't do anything right with him the last day or two——' He broke off. 'I'll carry the guitar for you.'

'I thought,' she teased him gently, 'that you told me Nick was a wonderful boss? The best?'

'That,' Paul said darkly, 'was before the carload of wine-growers and that reporter showed up. Ever since then there's just no pleasing him. "Do this, do that——" He's going around with a face like thunder. I just keep out of his way if I can. You don't know how lucky you are,' he said morosely, 'getting away from him tomorrow!'

Lucky! Sarah said the word silently.

They moved along the rough road to turn in at the wide-open gates. 'We used to go through the fence from Sunvalley before Bill put up the high black mesh netting shelterbelt against the winds,' Kate murmured. 'My goodness, there's a crowd here tonight!' For the road skirting the dark-stained timber house was lined with cars and pick-ups, trucks and vans.

Stereo music pulsed out through the open doorway as they reached the wide veranda, and Penny and Bill ushered the little group inside.

'Give me the guitar.' Penny whisked it away into a bedroom, then they were moving into the familiar lounge where white sheepskin rugs had been rolled out of the way and on the polished floor couples were dancing to the insistent beat of a hit tune that had been a top favourite in the pop music world at the time when Sarah had left London. Would Nick ask her to dance with him tonight? At that moment, as if drawn by a magnet, she found herself meeting his smouldering dark eyes. He was standing among a group of men at the back of the room, and her heart did a crazy somersault. Lean, strong, tanned, with deep smile-lines carved down either side of his face. But he wasn't smiling now. At last she wrenched her glance aside, realised that guests were moving towards her, and the next moment she was surrounded by groups of well-wishers.

'How about a dinner date in London next week?' called a lively masculine voice, and she glanced up to see a tall, gangling figure making his way through the throng in her direction.

'Larry!' she said in surprise as he came to join her. 'I haven't seen you for ages.'

'And whose fault is that? Each time I've rung you you've turned me down——'

'I know, I know. But I didn't dream you'd be here tonight. You live so far away, and I know your microlight——'

'Doesn't function at night.' His boyish tones deepened. 'Nothing on earth would have kept me away! Am I glad I got word over the grapevine that you were off back to England all of a sudden! I sure broke some speed records on the road to make it in time to get here tonight, but it was worth it!' Young and happy and uncomplicated, he caught her hand in his and guided her through the chattering groups towards the cleared dance space in the centre of the room.

'Have I got news for you!' Larry's freckled face was alight with excitement. 'Wait for it! I'm taking off on the plane for London myself next week! I've been promising myself a trip to England for ages, and——' his arm tightened around her slim waist '—is this the moment!'

Sarah, however, was no longer listening. She was conscious only of Nick's hard stare. He was standing at the bar among a group of men, a glass held in his hand, his mouth set in a straight line.

As the hours went by she felt as though she was moving in a dream. Larry scarcely left her side, and his high spirits left no doubt that he had no suspicion of her own lack of interest in all he was confiding to her of his life, his work and plans for joining her in London in a short time.

All the time tension was building up inside her. It was long past midnight and she was desperately wondering how she could make an announcement herself when a masculine voice called through the laughter and chatter, 'How about a song, Sarah? Just something to remember you by?'

It was the perfect opportunity for her to put her plan into action. Maybe, just maybe, tonight fate was on her side. Throwing a brilliant smile round the waiting groups, she called back, 'A pleasure.' Her heart was beating twenty to the dozen and she dared not glance in Nick's direction. 'I'll get my guitar.'

Bursts of applause followed her as she turned and slipped away. Soon she was whipping her muslin blouse over her head, unzipping her skirt with shaking fingers. Then, taking the European-style dress from the guitar case where she had hidden it, she drew the soft folds of cotton over her shoulders. A quick check in the mirror made her catch her breath in delighted surprise. The traditional Yugoslav costume could have been made for her, its soft pink shadings and style subtly flattering to her dark hair and cheeks now flushed with excitement. She took one last glance in the mirror. Now for her chance of gaining a lifetime of happiness with the man she loved! It might work. She drew a deep breath. She would *make* it work!

The crowd fell silent as she went back into the big room and took the centre of the floor, smiled around her, then began plucking the strings of the instrument. Could this be the way gamblers felt when they risked everything they valued on a single throw of the dice? Don't look at Nick, not yet!

The next moment the clink of glasses was stilled and her voice, clear and strong, rose on the air in a ballad of the gum-diggers of a century earlier.

As her voice died into silence a thunderous applause broke out around her and she looked directly at Nick. But he didn't appear to be the same man he had been earlier in the evening. Nick with tiny lamps burning deep in his dark eyes. And the way he was gazing at her... The next moment he was striding purposefully through the groups as he made his way towards her.

He reached her side a split-second before Larry, and she caught the other man's look of surprise followed by disappointment. Then she forgot everything else in the world but Nick. Someone had put a tape on the stereo and the rhythm of an old-fashioned waltz drifted through the room.

He swept her into his arms, and as they moved away together Sarah felt a wild, sweet happiness surging through her. Faces around her blurred out of focus, and nothing in all the world mattered but being enfolded in Nick's arms, blissfully, where she belonged.

In silence they circled the dance-floor, then Nick guided her out through the french doors and, taking her hand in his, drew her down the steps and out into the darkness of the star-strewn night. In the shadows of tall trees he took her in his arms, gathered her close and lowered his seeking lips to hers. 'I love you.' His tones were husky with emotion.

'Love you, Nick,' she whispered. Tremors of excitement were pulsing their way through her body as she responded to the heady excitement of his kiss. When she could speak once again she said softly, 'You remembered——?'

'My darling——' tenderly he cupped her face in his hands '—I never forget anything about you. I've loved you from the first moment I met you——'

'Even,' she teased gently, 'when you discovered who I really was?'

'All the time.' All at once his deep tones were unsteady. 'I've been going through hell these last few weeks. I thought I'd never see you again, that you were leaving me for ever——'

'I thought you didn't want me here.'

'Didn't want *you*, my darling?' To make certain she fully understood his feelings for her, his lips found hers in a caress that sent her senses spinning. 'I'll never let you go! I want you right here beside me. We'll make a great team, you and I. Maybe,' he whispered against her lips, 'after a while not just you and I. You know what I told you about wine-making——'

Sarah raised a tremulous face to his. '"To achieve perfection,"' she quoted softly, '"whatever is done with wine should be done with love."'

When at last they made their way back to the crowded room Sarah's face was flushed, her eyes brilliant, and she looked like a girl who had just been thoroughly kissed and didn't care who knew it! All that mattered to her was Nick, his vibrant tones laced with barely concealed excitement as he drew her forward with him to face the onlookers.

'Special announcement, folks!' His arm tightened around her shoulders. 'I've got news for you! Sarah's not leaving Sunvalley tomorrow after all. She's staying right here with me!' His words fell into a startled silence.

'We're planning to be married quite soon, and you're all invited to the wedding——'

His voice was drowned by the chorus of cheering and congratulations that echoed around them. Through a gap in the groups Sarah caught a glimpse of Larry's stricken face. He sent her a twisted smile, then flung around to disappear from sight among the crowd.

The next moment she forgot everything else in a haze of happiness as glasses clinked together and friendly voices rose all around her.

'To Nick and Sarah!'

4 FREE

Romances and 2 FREE gifts just for you!

You can enjoy all the heartwarming emotion of true love for FREE! Discover the heartbreak and the happiness, the emotion and the tenderness of the modern relationships in Mills & Boon Romances.

We'll send you 4 captivating Romances as a special offer from Mills & Boon Reader Service, along with the chance to have 6 Romances delivered to your door each month.

Claim your FREE books and gifts overleaf...

The truth often hurts . . .

Sometimes it heals

Critically injured in a car accident, Liz Danvers insists her family read e secret diaries she has kept for years – revealing a lifetime of courage, acrifice and a great love. Liz knew the truth would be painful for her aughter Sage to face, as the diaries would finally explain the agonising choices that have so embittered her most cherished child.

Available now priced £4.99

WORLDWIDE

Available from Boots, Martins, John Menzies, W.H. Smith and other paperback stockists.

Also available from Mills and Boon Reader Service, P.O. Box 236, Thornton Road, Croydon, Surrey CR9 3RU

Next Month's Romances

Each month you can choose from a wide variety of romance with Mills & Boon. Below are the new titles to look out for next month, why not ask either Mills & Boon Reader Service or your Newsagent to reserve you a copy of the titles you want to buy – just tick the titles you would like and either post to Reader Service or take it to any Newsagent and ask them to order your books.

Please save me the following titles:	Please tick	√
AN OUTRAGEOUS PROPOSAL	Miranda Lee	
RICH AS SIN	Anne Mather	
ELUSIVE OBSESSION	Carole Mortimer	
AN OLD-FASHIONED GIRL	Betty Neels	
DIAMOND HEART	Susanne McCarthy	
DANCE WITH ME	Sophie Weston	
BY LOVE ALONE	Kathryn Ross	
ELEGANT BARBARIAN	Catherine Spencer	
FOOTPRINTS IN THE SAND	Anne Weale	
FAR HORIZONS	Yvonne Whittal	
HOSTILE INHERITANCE	Rosalie Ash	
THE WATERS OF EDEN	Joanna Neil	
FATEFUL DESIRE	Carol Gregor	
HIS COUSIN'S KEEPER	Miriam Macgregor	
SOMETHING WORTH FIGHTING FOR	Kristy McCallum	
LOVE'S UNEXPECTED TURN	Barbara McMahon	

If you would like to order these books in addition to your regular subscription from Mills & Boon Reader Service please send £1.70 per title to: Mills & Boon Reader Service, P.O. Box 236, Croydon, Surrey, CR9 3RU, quote your Subscriber No:.................................... (If applicable) and complete the name and address details below. Alternatively, these books are available from many local Newsagents including W.H.Smith, J.Menzies, Martins and other paperback stockists from 12th February 1993.

Name:..

Address:..

....Post Code:...............................

To Retailer: If you would like to stock M&B books please contact your regular book/magazine wholesaler for details.

You may be mailed with offers from other reputable companies as a result of this application. If you would rather not take advantage of these opportunities please tick box ☐